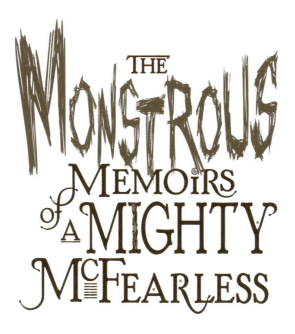

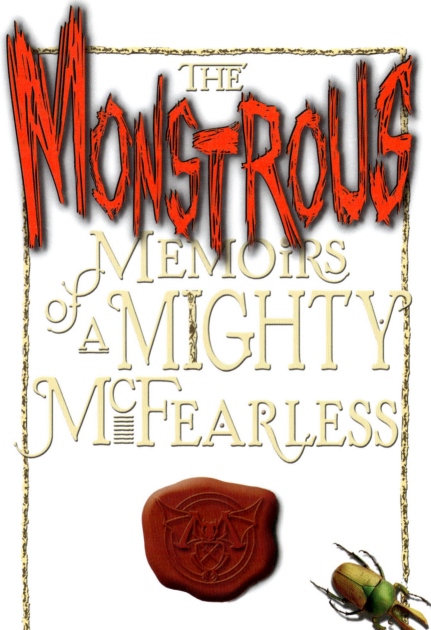

THE MONSTROUS

MEMOIRS OF A MIGHTY McFEARLESS

BY AHMET ZAPPA

MONSTER DESIGNS AND ILLUSTRATIONS BY AHMET ZAPPA
PHOTO ILLUSTRATIONS AND SCULPTURES BY CLAY SPARKS
PHOTOGRAPHS OF MAIN CHARACTERS BY BRIAN BOWEN-SMITH
COSTUME DESIGN BY PARIS LIBBY

RANDOM HOUSE 🏠 NEW YORK

Published in the United States by Random House Children's Books, a division of Random House, Inc., New York.

RANDOM HOUSE and colophon are registered trademarks of Random House, Inc.

Grateful acknowledgment is made to the following for permission to reproduce previously published material: Hemera Technologies, Inc.: for the use of Photo Objects from THE BIG BOX OF ART. © Hemera Technologies, Inc.; and Zappa Family Trust: for the use of Frank Zappa images. © 1967, 1984, 2006 Zappa Family Trust. Used by permission.

Cover design by Tanya Mauler.

www.randomhouse.com/kids

Library of Congress Cataloging-in-Publication Data
Zappa, Ahmet.
The monstrous memoirs of a mighty McFearless / written and illustrated by Ahmet Zappa.
    p. cm.
SUMMARY: With the help of Mr. Devilstone and a book called the Monstranomicon, Minerva and her brother Max go to the evil Zarmaglorg's Castle Doominstinkinfart to rescue their father, who they have discovered comes from a long line of monsterminators.
ISBN 0-375-83287-4 (trade)
[1. Monsters—Fiction. 2. Brothers and sisters—Fiction.
3. Adventure and adventurers—Fiction.] I. Title.
PZ7.Z258Mon 2006
[Fic]—dc22
2005025828

PRINTED IN CHINA
10 9 8 7 6 5 4 3 2 1
First Edition

For my future child. Just the idea of you
puts the biggest smile on my face.
I can't wait to meet you and to bite your little feet.

Wake Up, McFearless

$\mathcal{M}$aybe it was the smell of the Snargle's horrible breath, blowing from its rancid, rotten, razor-toothed mouth. Or was it the horribly loud *clang, crash* and *clunk* that thundered from the Snargle's slithery snout that woke me? Yes, that was it. It was a sort of twelve-human-skulls-tumbling-together-inside-a-barrel-barreling-down-a-rocky-mountainside noise that filled the evil cavern.

Either way, there's really nothing worse than a snoring, overweight Snargleflougasaurus, its lizardlike, spotted, yellowish belly rising and falling with each stinky breath. Ugh. It's like a poisonous soufflé made with the world's most vile ingredients.

As my eyes adjusted to the smoky darkness, I realized there was one thing far worse than a Snargleflougasaurus: finding my bruised and bloody father locked in a giant ironclad birdcage suspended over a bottomless pit of fiery molten lava.

That's definitely worse.

Did I mention that my little brother, Max, and I were trapped in a giant ironclad birdcage too? It was terrible. Even though I am a McFearless, I have to admit that I was pretty scared. I had to find a way to get us out of there before it was too late. The fate of my family—and possibly the world—was at stake.

Calm down. Deep breath in, deep breath out. I've got to relax. Deep breath in. I can do this, I told myself.

My name is Minerva McFearless. I live at 1523 Rockinghorse Lane in Whistlesqueak. I'm eleven years old, and these are the things I can do:

1) I can read and write in Monstrosity, which is very exciting because Monstrosity is the secret language that all monsters use to communicate, and it's the oldest language on the planet. Unfortunately, I'm not so good at speaking Monstrosity. It sounds like I'm trying to gargle two starving miniature weasels desperately fighting over a half-filled tin can of peanuts.

2) I can do a one-handed cartwheel into a round-off, usually on the first try.

3) Without bragging, I'm a really smart kid. And I am great at geography. I can name all of Whistlesqueak's surrounding cities within a three-hundred-mile radius in alphabetical order, starting with the picturesque palazzi of Applelonia and going all the way up to the haunted hillsides of Zarmevil. In fact, there are 208 cities, to be precise. And if I wanted to, I could name them all backward. My dad is always telling me I'm too smart for my own good and that's why I'm always getting into trouble.

My nine-year-old brother, Maxwell McFearless, on the other hand, is one of the most annoying brats on the planet. Here are some very good reasons for saying so:

1) He likes to pull my hair.
2) He chews with his mouth open, and food bits are always flying out. It's so gross.
3) He's constantly digging holes in our backyard and burying my stuffed animals against their will. In fact, he has transformed our backyard into a dreadful cemetery. On rainy  days, you can see tiny, stuffed, fuzzy hands sticking out of muddy, soaked graves. Every time I go out there, I imagine their cute yet ghostly voices calling out to me:

"Why didn't you save us, Minerva? How could you let Max do this to us, Minerva? We'll never forgive you for this, Minerva. Never."

Unfortunately, my diabolical brother mixed horse manure into the dirt, so digging up my animals is out of the question. My father told me he'd make Max dig them out and wash them, but I'm afraid of poop germs. I feel so guilty. It makes me want to punch Max right in the face. He makes it hard for me to love him, but I do. Because, for better or worse, he's my little brother, and there's nothing I can do to change that.

However, I do feel that it's my job as an older sister to give Max equal parts love and torture, which I try to do on a regular basis.

At that moment, Max was next to me, lying facedown on the rusted floor of our filthy birdcage prison. His nose was two inches away from the monster flotsam of undigested bone fragments and other gross chunks of uneaten gore that littered our dangling domicile of death.

I could make out the bump on the back of his head, in the exact spot where the Snargle had clobbered him with its tail. The swollen lump on my own cranium was throbbing and pounding something awful. If Max's head felt half as bad as mine, he was really going to hate it when I woke him up.

By pinching him really hard.

Really, *really* hard.

Look, I know what you're thinking. How could I be so cruel? What if the Snargle heard his cries of pain and turned its attention toward us? Well, the truth is . . . Snargleflougasauri are notorious for their deafness, and it was time for Max to wake up.

Plus, I'll take any opportunity I can get for a little revenge.

"Max, wake up," I whispered soothingly as I squeezed a sensitive patch of skin (just below his armpit) with my fingernails.

"*Ow!* Why'd you do that?" Max yelped.

"Stuffed animals," I replied.

"Arghh, my head," Max moaned, rubbing his little scalp all over. He focused his bleary eyes on me. "I can't believe you pinched me. What's wrong with you?"

"I had to wake you up somehow, didn't I?"

Max scowled. Then a winning thought seemed to come to his criminal mind.

"That didn't hurt me at all, *Mini,*" Max taunted.

"It did too, you liar," I answered, instantly annoyed.

"No, it didn't, *Mini,*" Max said.

"Max, stop calling me that!" He knows I hate it when he calls me Mini. I'm a year and two months older than Max, but he's two inches taller. I hate being bigger but smaller!

Life is so cruel. Maybe I should have pinched him again.

"Minerva? Max! Is that you?" Our father's weary voice brought Max and me to instant attention. "I thought I'd never see you again."

"Oh, Daddy, are you okay?" I cried.

"I'm a little banged and bruised, but I'll survive."

"Well, don't worry, we're gonna get you out of

here," Max said . . . and then he whispered to me, "Won't we, Minerva?"

"No!" snapped my father. "I don't want you kids doing anything. It's too dangerous. Hold tight. I'll find a way to get us all out of here somehow."

"But, Dad, we can do it. We're tough," I said with a great deal of determination.

"Yeah, we made it here all by ourselves," bragged Max, looking a little upset by our father's lack of confidence in us.

"And we even fought monsters," I added huffily.

"Listen to me, children. I know you both think that you know what you're doing. But trust me, you have no idea what we're up against here. A creature

unlike any other, the most vilely vile, the most horribly horrible, the most murderously murderous monster of them all."

I gasped. "You don't mean—"

"Yes," our father replied. "The *Zarmaglorg*—the king of evil. And we're deep within the demonic depths of Castle Doominstinkinfart—a place no mortal has ever escaped."

"Oh, no!" Max and I cried.

"Oh, yes. I'm afraid it's true. He has been torturing me nonstop ever since I got here. He desires the evil magic held within the Enotslived Diamond." I suddenly realized that my father—the magnificent Manfred McFearless, the most McFearless man in the world—was scared.

Not good at all, I thought.

"Mini, Dad, you might want to see this," sputtered Max. He poked his head through the iron bars of our cage and pointed at the fiery pit below.

A millisecond later, an explosion of tremendous fury burst from the odious depths. The blast sent our cages crashing into each other, smashing Max and me into the bars of our hanging prison. We were tossed about like two unlucky kittens zipped inside a suitcase mercilessly dropped off a cliff. I was thrown into the rusted lock of our cage door, knocking all the air out of my lungs. And Max whacked his jaw so hard that I was sure he

had shattered all his teeth. A cacophony bounced around the stalactites that hung from the cavern ceiling. Massive swarms of unhappy bats detached themselves from their cozy hiding places and flew around us in a panicked frenzy.

Thirteen more massive balls of billowing fire erupted from the chasm below. Flames licked angrily at the cave walls and flew right past our cage, singeing the hairs off my brother's head. The smell of brimstone, burnt hair and fried bats was too much to bear, even for a McFearless.

Then, just as quickly as it had started, the quaking and baking stopped. For the time being, we were spared the cruel fate of being broiled alive. I determined three things as soon as the smoke cleared:

1) We were still breathing. (Good.)
2) The lock on our cage was busted. (Really good.)
3) The Snargle was finished with its nap. (Not so good.)

Missing Molly

I think that before I tell you what happened next, I should explain some things that happened two years before. It was on the anniversary of my mother's death that Max and I discovered just how not normal our family is. And this is where I think the story really ought to begin.

It was a very scary and cold night on Rocking-horse Lane. The sky was an awful black, swirling with sinister, grayish clouds. Heavy sheets of rain fell hard upon the rooftop of our home. The surrounding trees cast menacing shadows and would sometimes lose their gnarled, fingerlike branches as they eerily danced to the howling winds. Bright slashes of crackling lightning could be seen from every window. Even though Max and I were safe and dry inside, we felt every rumbling thunderclap vibrate through our bones. It was a spooky night to be left alone, but I told myself that I was a tough kid and my father would be home soon.

To keep warm, Max and I headed upstairs to sit by the fireplace in the library. That's my favorite room in the house. There are hundreds of books, maybe even thousands of them, crammed from floor to ceiling into thirty-foot-high wooden bookcases. A jam-packed collection, ranging from fact to fiction, modern to medieval, comedy to tragedy and mystery to history. There are massive leather-bound dictionaries in strange languages, which weigh a ton, and huge atlases containing maps of places I hope to explore someday.

My happiest memories of my mother, Molly Adelaide McFearless, take place in the library. She also loved that room. I can still see her hazel-brown eyes; her soft, dark hair; her thin, pretty nose and

her smiling lips, full of kisses. She used to sit in her favorite green velvet chair by the fire, directly under a very creepy oil painting of my great-great-great-grandfather—Maximillius McFearless. That's where I like to sit now. She'd read lots of stories to us, and we'd laugh at the funny voices she'd create for all the strange people who lived inside the pages of the books. She exposed us to complicated mathematical equations and astonishing scientific texts with expertly drawn images of amazing animals, bizarre birds and peculiar plant life. (These were my favorites.) She told us tales about brave and adventurous sea captains who had battled giant waves, aboard cannon-firing pirate ships, in search of glorious golden treasures. (These were Max's favorites and what I like to call silly little boy stuff.)

Another reason I love the library is its magnificently painted ceiling depicting a magical midnight sky filled with faraway stars, bright moons and dazzlingly colored planets. When Max was three years old, my mother climbed up one of the tall, rickety old library ladders with a paintbrush in one hand and a palette of paints in the other. Barefooted, on the highest rung, she scanned the frescoed cosmos for the perfect place to start painting. Balancing herself precariously, she dipped her paintbrush in gold and stretched up on the tips of her toes. The ladder wobbled beneath her ever so slightly as she started to paint.

"Minerva," she said as droplets of gold fell onto her cheek. "Did you know that I started this tradition when you were born?"

I shook my head.

"Well, I did. You were my inspiration. Do you know which one I painted for you?"

"No," I said as I watched the ancient ladder shake under the strain of my mother's weight.

"Right there," she said, pointing at a beautiful pinkish constellation of eight vibrant stars that formed a perfect heart around one ruby-red sparkling sun in the middle.

"You, my little Minerva, are the one in the center. Can you see it, the red one surrounded by eight guiding stars?"

I did see it, and I loved it.

"Eight is the number of forever, and that's how long I'm going to love you, Minerva. Forever." Then she blew me a kiss and went back to work.

I was getting very nervous, but she didn't seem to care or notice how much the ladder groaned. She merrily continued her painting, each brushstroke purposely placed and gracefully executed, until at last she was finished.

"Voila! Minerva, what do you think?" she asked. "It's a comet for Max with a golden shimmering tail for my golden boy."

I told her I liked it, but really I didn't. I liked *my* constellation better.

Flop, crick, flop, crack, flop, creak. I crossed my fingers as she descended the dangerous ladder. Once safely on the floor, she hurried toward me, grabbed me in her loving arms and showered me with endless kisses. That was my last happy moment with her alive. She died a couple of days later.

(Mom, if you can read this all the way from heaven, I want you to know that I really miss you, Dad misses you, and Max is a jerk, but he misses you too.)

Like I said, it was the anniversary of my mother's death, and my father likes for this to be

a day of celebration. So every year, just like he used to do for my mother's birthday, my father rides the same horse down the same stretch of road to the same bakery and buys the same incredibly yummy seven-layer grapefruit cake with the best cream cheese frosting ever (my mother's favorite). Then we throw a little family party for just the three of us in honor of her passing.

After putting on his rain gear and his riding boots, my father squeezed us both tightly. He kissed us each on the forehead and told us that he'd be back in time for dinner. Then he gave us the rules:

1) Lock the doors behind him.
2) Be nice to each other.
3) Above all else, stay out of trouble.

Then off he went, galloping down the muddy road, in the middle of a terrible storm, for his Molly.

The Trouble with Trouble

𝒩ow, being the good children that we are, we did as we were told. We locked the doors behind him. We were being nice to each other (which is rare). But the trouble with trouble for Max and me is that more often than not, if we're left alone, we find trouble.

Let me explain. Getting into trouble and finding trouble are two very different things.

Getting into trouble is when you knowingly do something you know you shouldn't do.

For example, I intentionally pushed my bratty brother down a flight of stairs in hopes that it would knock some sense into him. I know that I'm older and I should know better than to push Max down an entire flight of stairs. I'm not going to lie and say that it didn't feel good to see him toppling head over heels, smashing and crashing all the way to the bottom step and landing with a nice ear-pleasing thud. And I'm not going to say that

I'm happy he suffered no injuries or broken bones. But I will say that he blew a massively disgusting, embarrassing snot bubble out of his left nostril while crying his eyes out and screaming at the top of his lungs. Now, I know that this sounds harsh, but in my defense and for the record, it was an act of justifiable retaliation for the heinous acts of cruelty that I endure on a daily basis. You see, my brother, Tyrannosaurus Max, purposely shattered my small handblown glass baby rabbit figurine for no reason. An item of mine that I happened to be extremely fond of. Just so you know, I was severely punished. I wasn't allowed to play outside or leave the house for a whole two weeks in the middle of summer.

Finding trouble, on the other hand, is when you unknowingly do something you didn't know you shouldn't do.

For example:

Max and I were reading leisurely by the fireplace in the library, surrounded by candlelight, all warm and toasty, waiting for our father's return. Max was sprawled out on the dark wood floor with his head in some pirate book. He had one finger up his nose, enjoying a good pick, and his other hand was incessantly twirling his stupid marble. He never goes anywhere without it, for some lame reason, and every time he reads about pirates or pretends to be a pirate, he makes believe that it's a priceless jewel from his secret pirate chest: "Behold the Jewel of Bebladar. Only a mighty pirate king such as myself could have found such a wondrous beauty. With this priceless gem, I shall buy a fleet of pirate ships and sail away upon the treacherous seas of greed in search of my pirate destiny."

He is so annoying.

Meanwhile, I was in my mother's favorite chair, trying my hardest to stay focused on a fascinating zoological study on the trials and tribulations of raising an abandoned newborn vampire bat. But that night, for some reason, I couldn't stop staring at the creepy painting of Maximillius McFearless directly above me. I think I've always been freaked out by it because Max kind of resembles him in a weird sort of way. Well, except for one big difference—Max has two eyes and Maximillius has only one, with an eye patch where the other should be.

Suddenly—*"Burrrahhurrrp!"*—an impressively long and loud strawberry juice-induced belch blasted out of my brother's mouth. Thankfully, it took my mind off the creepy painting of Maximillius. But unluckily, Max's burp smelled like a fruity combination of rotten sausages and lumpy sour milk. It couldn't have been more gross! (But, I hate to admit, it was funny at the same time.) It smelled so bad, I had to get out of the library. I decided I was thirsty for a glass of water. So I stood, picked up the nearest lit candle and on the way out the door noticed that the fire needed another log or two. I asked Max to take care of it, and he gleefully accepted the task, which was nice because he hardly ever says yes to the things I ask him to do.

In the kitchen, I grabbed my favorite glass from the cupboard (the one with a squirrel holding an umbrella on it, which I love for its silliness). I turned on the faucet, and the pipes hissed ominously as I filled my glass to the rim. All of a sudden, I felt like the shadows were closing in on me. I started getting scared. I really wanted to be back upstairs with Max and the safe feel of my mother's chair, so I gulped my water down as quickly as I could.

"Minerva!" my little brother screamed from the library. My heart almost leapt out of my chest. I momentarily choked and spit water all over the place.

"Come quick!" he screamed. "Minerva! Hurry!"

"I'm coming, Max! Hold on!" I yelled back with a cough. I ran as fast as I could. I had to save my baby brother from goodness-only-knew-what.

"Mini, where are you?" he cried out.

I charged up the stairs, taking them two by two. "I'm almost there, Max. I'm coming!" I hollered, and burst through the library doors, not knowing what I'd find.

Max was standing under our ancestor's portrait with a huge mischievous grin plastered

on his face. Nothing whatsoever was wrong with him. No danger in sight. What was he playing at?

"Max, you jerk, I was worried sick that something terrible was happening to you," I snarled at him. "Why do you always play these stupid tricks on me? I really thought you were in trouble!"

Max pointed at the fireplace. "Minerva, will you please just shut up and turn your head and look?"

In an instant my fear and anger were replaced with total shock. Right where the fireplace used to be was a massive pair of ivory-colored stone doors with the words "ALL MONSTERS BEWARE, FOR ONLY A MCFEARLESS MAY ENTER HERE" carved just above their two oversized solid-gold handles.

"What did you do, Max?" I asked, baffled.

"Come on, Mini! Let's see what's inside," he said, without answering my question.

"Where did the fireplace go? Max, how did this happen?"

"You're not going to believe this, Mini," Max began. "I went to place some more wood on the fire like you asked me to do. But then this weird red moth started flying around my face, so I grabbed the fire poker and pretended like it was a pirate sword and swung at the blasted moth a few times, but I missed and accidentally slammed the tip of the poker into a brick at the top of the fireplace. And I noticed that the brick moved, so I pushed on it a little more and—*poof*—the fire went out and those big doors appeared!" Max looked very satisfied.

I was stunned by what I'd just heard, and at the same time jealous that it wasn't my discovery. If this isn't a perfect example of finding trouble, then I don't know what is. I knew that our father probably wasn't going to be happy about this, but I just had to see what was inside.

Max and I placed our hands upon the golden handles of the mammoth doors. They felt cool and, to my surprise, gave way easily. We pushed the doors open and gained entry to a room that would forever change the destiny of our lives. Together we stepped into our family's mysterious past—and into our own dangerous future.

Monstranomicon

Smoky torches lined the secret passageway Max and I found ourselves cautiously following. The sounds of our footsteps and our breathing echoed eerily. Arcane symbols and scary images of horrible beasts attacking frightened, helpless families were etched into the walls all around us. When our teeth began to chatter, Max and I stopped and exchanged looks. We almost turned back. But instead we nodded silently, swallowed our fear down hard, grabbed each other's hands tightly, and bravely continued forward. The air was musty, like the way I imagined a tomb to smell. And the longer we walked, the worse it became. Various venomous spiders detached themselves from their dusty, sticky, wobbly webs once they saw us coming. I worried that they would leap out at us and sink their tiny poisonous fangs into our flesh. But instead, they quickly crawled away.

After walking for what seemed like forever,

Max and I stumbled upon yet another stone door. This one, however, was blood-red and much smaller than the last pair, and it had a very different ominous message carved just above its rusted doorknob.

"MCFEARLESSLY ENTER ONLY THOSE WHO ARE BRAVE, FOR THE KNOWLEDGE YOU FIND HERE YOU MUST MCFEARLESSLY TAKE TO YOUR GRAVE." Max read the words aloud and then frantically rifled through his pant pockets.

"Are you all right, Max? We don't have to go any further. We can turn around right now if you want to," I whispered.

"No, I'm fine, Minerva," Max replied in a transparent tough-guy-sounding voice. "Why would I want to do that?"

Obviously, I've known Max for a long time, and I've noticed two things about my little brother that only a big sister with a superb, scientific, sleuthlike mind, such as me, could detect.

1) Whenever he feels comfortable and happy, eventually his fingers go fishing for fresh booger trout up his nose.
2) Whenever he is uncomfortable and scared, eventually his fingers go fishing for a gum ball in hopes that he'll be able to chew all his fears away.

In the blink of an eye, Max plopped a pink gum ball into his mouth and began to chew it like a maniac. After only a few seconds, a visible sense of calm came over him. He moved up to the door and, with a gross, sloppy-slushy-sounding wet mouth, said, "I'm ready—if you are, Minerva."

"Okay, on the count of three," I responded, and put my hand right next to his on the doorknob. Then we looked at each other and readied ourselves for a nice twist of the knob.

"One, two, three!"

The door flew open and we went flying. Stupidly, Max and I had pushed way too hard, and we collided with a table full of terrifying things. Luckily, we survived the incident with only minor scrapes and scratches. But the table we connected with toppled over, its contents crashing to the floor with a boom. We picked ourselves up from the mess we'd made and surveyed our surroundings for the first time.

Max and I couldn't believe our eyes. It was like being in a museum full of things that weren't supposed to exist. Lanternlike canisters filled with a glowing green type of phosphorus lined the walls, and a startling stained-glass window of a multicolored fire-breathing dragon helped to illuminate our unusual surroundings, bathing everything before us in an unnatural light. There were sarcophagi filled with skeletons and display cases containing other rotting remains. Some of the skeletons had wings or spiky tails. Others had razor-sharp antlers or large pointed horns. There were monster skulls with only one eye socket, and some with three or even more. Suspended from the ceiling was a jaw so enormous that Max and I gasped when we saw its petrifying, petrified pointed teeth. There was also an exceptionally long examining table covered with an odd array of interesting items, including a microscope with slides of blood I assumed came from different breeds of carnivorous creatures. There were dirty-looking bottles full of perplexing plant life and containers of coagulated liquids with living organisms struggling to swim inside them. The room made me feel like I had to go wash my hands instantly, for fear of possible germ contamination.

We had discovered a room specifically designed for and devoted to the scientific study of malevolent monsters. When Max noticed the weirdly shaped weapons of war and the badly battered battle armor stacked against the farthest wall of the study, he couldn't contain himself. It was a dream come true for him: he obviously thought he'd finally be able to get his grubby little hands on his very own pirate sword. But it didn't quite work out that way. Max grabbed one of the oddly shaped swords from the wall, but it slipped out of his hands and fell directly onto his right foot. It turns out that puny little boys who dream of owning their very own pirate sword simply aren't strong enough yet to even lift one. Luckily for him, it fell blade-side up so that only the hilt of the sword bashed his toes, making him scream at the top of his lungs. It was fantastic. He walked with a limp for at least three days after that.

Max and I began to scour the majority of the room's unsanitary but amazing monster paraphernalia. My head swam with unnerving questions. *Why on earth is there a place like this in our house? Who uses it? And what is it for?* While my unanswered questions swirled around in my McFearless mind, my eyes stumbled across something in the shadows toward the back of the room. Resting on a paradoxically plain pedestal was the most unique book I'd ever seen. I couldn't take my eyes off it. The book was rather large and covered in some sort of leathery animal hide that I'd never seen before. It was as if its embossed cover of deep browns and golden iridescent lettering was just waiting for me to open it, calling me to it. The closer I got, the greater was my need to read from its pages. I reached out my hand to pick it up. I was so close.

"Minerva, no! Don't touch that book!" screamed my father. But it was too late. The book had invitingly opened itself up to me and snapped closed around my outstretched hand, biting me with its poisonous paper teeth. The last thing I saw before I passed out was the book's mysterious title . . . *Monstranomicon.*

The Legend of
Maximillius
McFearless

I woke up in my bedroom, in my own bed, my father sitting by my side. He looked anxious at first, but as soon as he realized I was awake, a loving smile of relief came to his face. "Minerva, are you feeling better? Does it hurt badly?" he asked.

"Only a little bit," I lied. My hand felt like it had been stung by a thousand bees; lots of little paper cuts were all around my fingers and palm. I looked down at it and gasped. It had swollen to the size of a watermelon.

"Here, drink this," my father said, and offered me a cup of some kind of bizarre brew he had cooked up. After just a few sips of the hot licorice-like liquid, I began to feel much better. My pain and swelling started to ebb away, which put me in a much better state of mind for getting to the bottom of a couple of things I wanted explained.

"What happened, Daddy?" I asked.

"Well, it seems that you and little Maxwell dis-

covered my study and fooled around with things I wish you wouldn't have. Are you sure you're okay, Mini?"

"Why did that book hurt me?" I asked, and sipped some more. It was really yummy.

"You tried to pick up the Monstranomicon and she bit you," answered my father uneasily.

"What are you talking about? Since when do books bite people?"

"Actually, this book not only bites, she also talks."

"How can that be? Why do you even have a book like that, and why didn't you ever tell me that monsters existed? What's going on here, Dad?" I wanted answers.

"What's the best way to put this?" my father said, fumbling for his words. "I'm not what you would call a normal dad with a normal occupation. . . . I really hoped that you'd be older and that your mother would be here when I told you this—"

"Dad, just tell me already," I interrupted, frustrated.

"Okay, then. Minerva, I'm what you might call a monsterminator," he said, finally spitting the words out. It seemed like a weight had been lifted off his shoulders then, and the rest of what he had to say came out much more easily. "I help people with their monster-infestation problems. Just like my father did, and his father before him, and so on and so on. That book you tried picking up is the source of all our McFearless monsterminating monster knowledge, a living, breathing encyclopedia on all of monsterkind, containing information on all their strengths, but more important, their weaknesses. Her poisonous bite either kills her victims or grants them the ability to read and understand her pages. You're lucky you're a McFearless, or you'd probably be dead. Oh, and before I forget, she wanted me to apologize to you, on her behalf. She feels terrible for biting you, and she'll try never to do it again."

"Um, okay. Tell her apology accepted, I guess," I said, still very confused.

"I will. Interestingly, though, she said that by the way you tasted, she thinks the two of you could easily become friends. Apparently, she's quite fond of you, Minerva, and I'm not sure how I feel about that. Remember, she's a monster—albeit a monster who's been turned from bad to good. She's still a monster. So you are not to spend any time with her, okay?"

"Okay," I answered. He knew me so well. I couldn't wait to talk with her. "But, Dad, how does one get a book that's alive? And are there other books that won't try to kill you that contain the same kind of information?"

"No, actually, Minerva, that is the only book of its kind, and your great-great-great-grandfather Maximillius McFearless, rest his soul, died obtaining it. Legend has it, Maximillius sought to steal the book for the information it held inside, so that he could use its knowledge to protect the world from all monsterkind. Unfortunately, the book belonged to the king of evil—otherwise known as the dreaded Zarmaglorg. Maximillius, being McFearless, decided to sneak into the evil king's private lair and, while the beast lay sleeping, discovered something else rather unexpectedly. Right next to the Monstranomicon was the Zarmaglorg's most powerfully prized possession—the Enots-lived Diamond, the source of the Zarma-glorg's evil powers! Quickly and quietly, Maximillius snatched the diamond before moving toward the Monstranomicon, not knowing that the book was actually a monster itself—and therein lay his downfall. As the story goes, Maximillius became the first human ever to lay hands upon the Monstranomicon, and therefore the first human to receive her dreadfully painful bite.

"Upon hearing Maximillius's awful screams of agony, the king of evil opened his eyes to find Maximillius with his two most prized possessions clutched tightly in his hands, writhing in pain. It's not exactly clear what transpired next, which for us in the McFearless family has caused many heated debates over the years. Some have speculated that with the combined power of the Monstranomicon and the Enotslived Diamond, Maximillius was able to defeat the Zarmaglorg, thus ending his reign of terror for good—but in doing so sacrificed his own life. Others believe that since he was the first victim of the Monstranomicon's sting, she poisoned Maximillius to death, and that when the Zarmaglorg ate his remains, he was poisoned as well. I'm not sure I believe any one of those stories, but I can tell you one thing for certain: neither Maximillius nor the dreaded Zarmaglorg has been heard from since.

"One night, shortly after Maximillius's disappearance, the Monstranomicon, wrapped in Maximillius's cloak, was left on our doorstep in broad daylight with a letter explaining how dangerous she is and that only a truly fearless McFearless may read from her pages. Minerva, very bad things would happen if that book were ever to fall back into the hands of monsters. So for hundreds of years, our family has been safeguarding all of the deadly information that's held within her and has served as mankind's last line of defense against all monsterdom's vicious attacks."

"Okay, so let me get this straight," I said, a little doubtfully. "You're a monsterminator? Monsters really exist and our family has been fighting monsters for hundreds of years?"

"Yes, Minerva, it's all true," he answered.

My mind was spinning.

"So this is why you're always having to race off somewhere on a moment's notice? And why you sometimes disappear in the middle of the night without ever waking us to say goodbye?"

"Yes, Mini, and I'm sorry if you ever worried or wondered where I was," my father said. "I hated leaving you and Max, but I always made sure I left you in Randolph's safe hands." (Randolph Beesmilk has been my father's best—and I think only—friend for as long as I can remember. He has been looking after us more and more ever since my mother passed away.)

"I want to be a monsterminator," I announced proudly.

"Minerva, this is not a game. Monsters love to eat children and destroy people's lives. It's an incredibly hazardous job that only a grown-up—and I repeat, a *grown-up*—can handle."

"But, Dad, I'm a McFearless, and that's what McFearlesses do. We monsterminate," I said desperately.

"Now, I love you, Minerva, and I would do anything to keep my children safe. So listen to me. I don't want you or Max ever to go inside my study or try to read from that book again. Do you understand? It's dangerous and both of you could get seriously hurt in there."

The thought of not being allowed to go back in the monster-study room seemed like one of the worst things in the world to me. I couldn't let that happen. I needed a plan. I needed Max.

"This is not open for discussion, Minerva. You and Max are not allowed back in there. Do you understand me?" my father asked sternly.

"Yes, Dad," I said unhappily, with my fingers secretly crossed.

"Good," he said, and kissed my forehead. "Now that your hand is feeling better, let's go downstairs and have a piece of your mother's favorite grapefruit cake. Max is waiting."

Right Under His Nose

There was no stopping Max and me once we found out about our McFearless family secret and saw the amazing stuff our dad had in his hidden study. And we basically drove him nuts. We wanted to know everything there was to know about monsters and monsterminating. We couldn't stop ourselves from asking him questions all day long, and all he would ever say was "You're not old enough yet, Minerva," or "I'll tell you when you're older, Max," or "Please stop asking me about monsters. You are driving me insane!"

Those weren't good, scientific answers, so Max and I would just ask again and again.

"That's it, no chocolate or giggling allowed for five days," our father finally shouted.

Since he wouldn't give in to us, Max and I were left with no other choice. We developed a simple system in which one of us would occupy our father's time just long enough for the other to secretly steal another item from his definitely off-limits, super-secret monster study. And let me tell you, it worked flawlessly. We'd take things out and put them right back without him ever becoming the wiser.

Now, we love our father and hate disobeying him, but for two years, Max and I learned as much as we could behind his back. Every time our father would leave us to go on one of his monsterminating trips, Max and I would secretly rejoice. Sure, we'd miss him. And he'd always make certain that Randolph Beesmilk was there to keep a watchful eye on us. But good old Beezer didn't present too much of a challenge. Strangely, for a man who used to have loads of energy, Beezer seemed to fall asleep a lot those days. I wonder if it was because there were two McFearless children who had learned how to put odorless and tasteless things into his drinks that would knock him out? Now, I can neither deny nor confirm that, but I will admit that once Randolph was sleeping like a baby, Max and I would spend all day in our father's study, getting in some real quality monster-learning time. We learned many recipes from the Monstranomicon—and none of them were for chocolate chip cookies or custard pies. They were all recipes for monster maintenance and defending oneself against the creatures on her pages.

The Monstranomicon informed me that she pre-

ferred to be called *Ms.* Monstranomicon and that I should refer to her as such. I read page after page from the Monstranomicon, and we became fast friends. She even started to teach me how to speak in her native language, Monstrosity. She said that if I wanted to become a real monsterminator, I'd probably have to learn to speak it, and that I'd be the first female human ever to do so. She told me that it had been forbidden for her to teach any of us McFearlesses in the first place. Monster law states that monsters must never betray their own kind by teaching food (humans) their monster ways. Ms. Monstranomicon's biggest fear is that, one day, one of her monster relatives is going to find out what she's done and burn her alive, even though she's been hidden safely inside our house for years and years. I never told Max about any of this, because they were private girl conversations, just between friends.

After spending lots of time with Ms. Monstranomicon, I came to the conclusion that she was an incredible book who could do amazing things. For instance, if by accident one of her pages were ripped out, she could grow it back, just like a lizard can regrow its tail. She also loves to have her spine tickled, and one of her favorite things, besides biting hands, is when someone reads from her out loud. Even though she's my friend, and I do like to make my friends happy, translating for my bratty brother as I read from her was exhausting.

"Is there any way that you could allow Max to read from your pages without having to bite him first, Ms. Monstranomicon?"

"No, I think that I would not like to allow that. I want to bite him. He looks yummy. Honestly, I think he deserves a nice bite from me. You survived; chances are he will too," she said, shuffling her paper teeth around in her mouth while she talked. I explained all this to Max.

"So that's why her pages look all blurry when I try reading over your shoulder. Well, both of you can just forget it. There is no way I'm letting her bite me, Minerva," Max said nervously. "I remember how seriously swollen you got after she chomped down on you, and I'm not interested."

"You're a big chicken, Max, you know that? And you'll never be a proper monsterminator unless you let her," I said as I threateningly pushed Ms. Monstranomicon closer to his fingers. Max panicked and immediately put a green gum ball in his mouth.

"Minerva, k-k-keep that thing away from me," he stuttered.

I gave in to the fact that I'd be stuck reciting everything.

So I read chapter after chapter of Ms. Monstranomicon to Max, and together we studied up on spells and charms and the ingredients that went into them. We learned the names of the various types of monsters and how to tell them apart—which ones had fur, skin or scales, and which fiend's bite was deadly or would turn you into a monster yourself. Then I'd quiz Max and he'd do the same to me. We quickly became true monster experts.

Bewildered by a Box

*I*t simply showed up on our doorstep one night, no note, no messenger in sight. It was waiting there when the three of us came home from a nice late-night family dinner in town. The second Max and I spotted the strange box, we recognized it from the pages of the Monstranomicon. Of course, we couldn't let our dad know that, so we played dumb and asked him what he thought it might be. He uncomfortably said that it was "just an ugly wooden box, nothing to get excited over" and picked it up as fast as he could so that Max and I couldn't touch it.

"Can I have it, since you think it's so ugly and no big deal?" I asked.

He floundered for a bit and said, "No! It's probably a neighbor's, delivered here by accident. I'll check with the houses next door in the morning. Right now I want you kids to go upstairs and get ready for bed." My dad was a bad fibber, and Max

and I saw right through him. So we did as we were told, and he tucked us into our beds and kissed us good night. But the moment he left our rooms and headed for his study, Max and I met up to follow him. We both had the same questions: Why did our father react so strangely when he saw the Bewilder Box, and what monstrous thing could possibly be inside of it?

Okay, for those of you who don't know what a Bewilder Box is, I'll tell you. Bewilder Boxes are created for and used exclusively by monsters to keep their very most prized possessions safely hidden. Think of them as combination safes for monsters. No two are alike, and there's only one way to open a Bewilder Box. You have to know exactly where and in what sequence to touch its monster markings in order to open it. They're indestructible and impregnable otherwise. Bewilder Boxes are also creatively claw-manufactured by monster craftsmen named Loogos.

✦ THE LOOGO ✦

These lily-livered, long-necked, pointy-beaked monsters are not as scary as one might think. In fact, Loogos are shy and timid creatures who prefer working over wreaking havoc and going on destructive rampages like other monsters. They pride themselves on their monster craftsmanship and are the creative masterminds responsible for the invention of the Bewilder Box, as well as other important items currently used by monsters, such as Scale Shapers, Tail Lifters, Claw Scrapers, Fang Brushers and even False Fangs (for the older monster that has lost its teeth). Whatever contraption a monster may need, Loogos are the ones to build it. They use wood from only the finest and rarest of twigless monster trees for all their crafts. Strangely, Loogos don't enjoy eating human children, but instead prefer feasting on ponies or snacking on baby goats for sustenance.

A defensive recipe:
LIZARD LOZENGE TEA

You will need:

- 1 dirty old teacup
- 1 silver spoon to stir with
- 2 tablespoons of blackberry preserves
- 1 teaspoon of Earl Grey tea
- 7 tablespoons of cottage cheese
- 3 teaspoons of black ink
- 1 dead spider
- 1 bird feather

Put the blackberry preserves, Earl Grey tea, cottage cheese and black ink into the dirty old teacup. Stir the contents 11 times counterclockwise with the silver spoon and say these magic words: *Lollyrat, sugarhat, bifrica, zipple.* Next, add the dead spider and say these magic words: *Jailbop, vittenkrause, rimhornet, gankle.* Then add the bird feather, stir 11 times clockwise with the silver spoon and say these magic words: *Lizrump, lizrizzle, loogolozzle, brackmackle meazel, hot tea, not tea, loogolizard, go fizzle.* Place the Lizard Lozenge Tea at your front door to be Loogo-safe for 17 months. Ⓜ

My father was sitting at his desk under his stained-glass dragon window, looking through a magnifier, closely studying the markings on the box in total concentration. If he had discovered that we were spying on him, he'd probably have fed us to a gang of great white sharks.

As time passed, Max and I got pretty bored watching our father tinkering around with the box. We were just about to call it quits when all of a sudden my father proved once again that he's a McFearless genius. He had cracked the box's creature code! The Bewilder Box yawned open, its top half sliding smoothly away to reveal the prize hidden inside. We couldn't wait to see what he was going to pull out of it.

Sticking his fingers into the belly of the box, my father produced a scarlet diamond that was about

the same size as Max's stupid marble. The look on my father's face was one of total astonishment as he lifted the diamond up into the moonlight. "Could it really be, after all this time?" he said.

The second that the moon's rays touched the diamond's surface it began to glow as if it had caught on fire. "What strange forces are at work here? How did you find your way back into the hands of a McFearless? If, indeed, you are what I think you are, this can't be good."

"Minerva, keep your fingers crossed that Dad doesn't lock it back up inside the Bewilder Box before I get a chance to check it out," Max whispered very quietly. "I wonder how much it's worth and what kind of monster originally owned it. Do you think it was a Grumplemiser's?"

"No way, Grumplemisers normally have much bigger Bewilder Boxes and way bigger hoards to go in them," I whispered back to Max. "Plus, they usually only like precious metals, not gems. So my guess would be that it originally belonged to a Krunkadillion. Don't you remember that Krunkadillions like to use precious stones as replacement teeth to feel prettier when looking in the mirror?"

"Yeah, you're probably right, Mini. I forgot about Krunkadillions," he admitted, sounding a little miffed that I was more likely correct than he was—which was very satisfying to me.

⋆✦ The Grumplemiser ✦⋆

These bad-tempered, flame-headed, turquoise-spotted, thieving beasts love to do only two things: steal precious metals (especially gold) and set fires. They are completely impervious to heat and fire. Chances are, if there's a house in flames, gold or other jewelry is being stolen by a Grumplemiser somewhere within the inferno. They really enjoy the taste of charred children (ones with gold-filled cavities being their favorites) as well as the flavor of boiling metal. Grumplemisers fill their oversized palms with the spoils of their thievery, hold the precious metals over their stove-top-like heads and melt them for a special treat to slurp upon. Most Grumplemisers prefer living close to mining towns or, in some cases, inside the gold mines themselves. They're well known for telling very bad jokes and are prone to severe back injuries. Wearing jewelry around a Grumplemiser is an almost surefire way to get yourself killed or, worse, roasted alive. They absolutely detest the ocean and hate most of all the sound of people chewing.

A defensive recipe:
FOOL'S GOLDEN FRIED CHICKEN SURPRISE ATTACK

You will need:

- 1 cauldron (or large mixing bowl)
- 1 wooden spoon
- 1 hammer
- 3 large sheets of aluminum foil
- 1/2 cup of orange juice
- 5 tablespoons of olive oil
- 10 teaspoons of salt
- 1 fried chicken breast
- 4 cloves of garlic
- 6 strawberries
- 12 tiny garden rocks
- 1 grape (or substitute 100 raisins)

Into your cauldron or large mixing bowl, pour the orange juice, olive oil and salt and beat together with the wooden spoon. Next, place the fried chicken breast, garlic, strawberries, tiny garden rocks and grape (or 100 raisins) in a pile on a hard flat surface. Then pick up your hammer and smash everything together. Once the mixture is properly smashed, scoop it up and place it inside your cauldron. Blend all the ingredients together with the wooden spoon and say these magic words: *Fire ribbit, gorgle piggit, fizer glandio floon. Goldy spigot, burning cricket, Grumplemiser sploom.* Next, place a healthy handful of the cauldron's contents into one of the large pieces of aluminum foil; then wrap it all up nice and tight like a baked potato. Repeat the process with the other pieces of foil. Now speak the final magic words: *Grumplemiser, Grumplemiser, Grumplemiser DOOM!* Place all 3 of these foiled pieces of doom in your mailbox for 2 nights and your house will be Grumplemiser-free for one year. If eaten by a Grumplemiser, a Fool's Golden Fried Chicken Surprise Attack will kill it within minutes. Ⓜ

✦ THE KRUNKADILLION ✦

These unfortunate-looking, snaggletoothed, hairless, purple-skinned, pig-snouted monsters are ferociously dangerous. They have highly unpredictable tempers and often lash out at unsuspecting victims with deadly force. Krunkadillions hate their physical appearance (especially their crooked smiles) and as a result prefer the darkness offered to them by the deepest parts of jungles. In false hopes of making themselves more attractive, a large majority of Krunkadillions rip out their own teeth and replace them with gorgeous sparkly diamonds, rubies or emeralds. Gemstone collecting is a favorite pastime for these beasts, and they'll go to any length to protect their hoards from thievery. Krunkadillions are tree-dwellers, and their oversized hands are perfectly designed for the scaling of any variety of tree. They are also terribly smelly creatures that reek like a baboon's backside on a hot day. Never tell a Krunkadillion that it is ugly, unless being murdered is your desired result.

A defensive recipe:

The Cat Hand of Doom

You will need:

- 1 cauldron (or large mixing bowl)
- 1 pair of human hands
- 1 left-hand leather glove
- 6 inches of twine
- 1 cup of used coffee grounds
- 1 teaspoon of maple syrup
- 1 cup of flour
- 1 cup of yogurt
- 1/3 cup of spoiled milk
- 1/3 cup of cat hair (any breed)
- 1 dirty radish

Place the coffee grounds, maple syrup and flour in your cauldron or large mixing bowl and mix together with human hands until properly blended. Say these magic words: *Moose, rubbish, bwing bwong bwang, alligator, crocodile, zwing zwong zwang.* Then add the yogurt, spoiled milk and cat hair to your cauldron. Mix everything until it becomes gross and clumpy. Next, fill the left-hand leather glove with the mixture, making sure to cram as much as you can into each finger. Once the glove is almost full, add the dirty radish. Tie the twine around the open end of the glove, double-knotting it tightly so that none of the contents can fall out. Say these magic words: *Krunk a dunk, flunk a skunk, dribble, drabble, you are so pretty, poop kerplunk.* Sleep with the Cat Hand of Doom under your pillow overnight and you'll be protected from Krunkadillions for 300 days. ▨

Max and I freaked when our dad suddenly stood up from behind his desk and headed straight toward our hiding spot. We thought we'd been discovered. Our hearts were pounding. Thankfully, the legendary Manfred McFearless sped right on by us.

Howleewoofed

*W*e crawled out from under our table and toward the Bewilder Box for a better look. Max began shaking the Bewilder Box like a madman in hopes of opening it. I barely heard the faint voice of Ms. Monstranomicon calling out my name. I scooted over to where she was sitting, on a shelf above my father's desk, and she informed me that she had watched the entire sequence my father had used to open the Bewilder Box. "I'd be willing to tell you exactly what to do—as long as Max would agree to let me bite him a little," Ms. Monstranomicon promised.

I never thought Max would go for it, not in a million years. But after I explained to him what she was offering, he quickly put a gum ball in his mouth, chewed it like it was his last and said he'd do it.

"Minerva, ask her to help you open it up first.

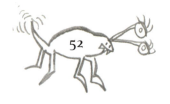

I don't really trust her," he said, shaking and chewing fearfully.

Before he'd even finished his sentence, Ms. Monstranomicon was telling me what to do. Max nervously handed me the Bewilder Box, and I followed her instructions precisely. Once again, the lid slid smoothly open, and before I even had a chance to reach inside, Max had snatched the scarlet diamond for himself.

"This is so amazing!" cried Max, staring at it like he was in a trance, befuddled by its beauty.

"Let me see it too, Max," I said.

"Wait a second, if I'm the one who's going to get chewed on by that book, then I'm definitely looking at this diamond first," Max whined.

He did kind of have a point. So, like a good big sister, I reminded him of his deal and held up Ms. Monstranomicon. "Fine, jerk, but she's hungry and you don't want to keep her waiting, do you?" I hoped that Ms. Monstranomicon would hurt my brother a million times worse than she had hurt me.

Max stuck his left hand out slowly toward Ms. Monstranomicon, and she shook ever so slightly in anticipation of a good meal. Gurgly stomach noises rumbled from somewhere down near her spine. I watched with a smile, knowing what sort of pain was in store for Max. Closer and closer he moved, until finally he placed his fingers between

her brightly colored pages. Nothing happened at first, but then—*slam!*—Ms. Monstranomicon clamped herself shut and bit down hard. Max let out a scream that could've curdled blood, but to my surprise, he didn't pass out like I had done. Still, his eyes did fill with tears, and his hand immediately began swelling.

"It feels awful, doesn't it, Max?" I couldn't resist a smile.

"Arghh! Yeah, it kills. Oh, it stings so bad," he moaned as he flapped his injured hand around.

"I'm glad."

I didn't have much time to enjoy the humor in Max's agony, because in the distance we heard our father's voice: "Max? Minerva?" Max and I were busted.

"We are in so much trouble, Max. There is no way we're going to get out of this one. Really ham up the fact that you're in pain, okay? If you pile it on thick enough, maybe we'll both escape his wrath."

"That won't be hard for me to do," moaned Max. I almost felt bad for him for a second.

"You should probably put the diamond back inside the box before Dad gets here," I told him.

Max attempted to place the diamond back inside the Bewilder Box, but his huge swollen hand kept getting in his way. I turned my head nervously toward the study entrance, watching for our father.

"Hurry!" I said, hearing our father's bootheels clonking on the passageway floor as he speedily moved toward us. "Max, close it!" Max finally slid the Bewilder Box shut with his good hand. I quickly grabbed it from him and put it back where we had found it on the desk. Father exploded through the doorway, startling both of us.

"Thank heavens you're all right," he said as he slammed the door and locked it. "I went looking for you everywhere, and when I couldn't find you, I prayed that somehow you'd both be down here." Max and I were stunned. Blood was smeared all over his shirt. "Children, help me barricade this door. Quickly, we don't have much time before they track my scent down and find their way in here."

The immediacy with which he spoke made us both instantly follow his orders and put a tremendous amount of fear into our hearts. We helped him pile as many things as we could grab against the door. "Why are you covered in blood? What's going on, Daddy?" I asked fearfully.

"We're under attack. Monsters have somehow discovered our McFearless home and have come for us. I fought one of them upstairs with a can opener, and it sliced me with its claw. I counted only three of them—a foul-breathed Snargleflougasaurus, a gargantuanly overweight Glorch and a seriously sticky Moldren. I should be able to handle them all with no problem now that I'm in here with all my monster-minational gear."

"How can we help, Dad?" asked Max, his big swollen hand hanging useless by his side.

"Listen to me. There is a trapdoor under my desk that leads down into a monster-proof room. I want you two to move my desk, grab the Monstra-nomicon and climb inside right now!" As he shouted instructions to us, my father ran to his monster-fighting arsenal at the far end of the room. He selected the weapons he thought he might need and suited up for battle. Max and I tried to move the desk, but it seemed like it weighed three hundred pounds. We couldn't push it even an inch.

BAM! BAM!! BAM!!! BAM!!!!

The menacing monsters had tracked us all down, and the door to the study was rocked by a flurry of powerful monster blows. Hammering claws raked at the stone door. It held fast, but it wouldn't for long. They wanted meat—McFearless meat—and the sounds of their jaws, hungrily chomping nothing, sent shivers down my spine.

"Daddy, we can't move it by ourselves!" I screamed as the pounding intensified and the monsters began growling menac-ingly.

"WE DON'T WANT TO HURT YOU,

MCFEARLESS. LET US IN. WE'RE ONLY GOING TO EAT YOU ALL UP," bellowed the Snargle-flougasaurus, the Glorch and the Moldren together. Their raspy monster voices sounded like an awful combination of fingernails being dragged down a chalkboard and the unbearable gurgling moo of a cow speared through its middle.

"OPEN THE DOOR! WE PROMISE NOT TO SUCK YOUR DELICIOUS BRAINS OUT THROUGH YOUR NOSE AND INTO OUR STARVING BELLIES. WE SWEAR WE WON'T GOBBLE YOU DOWN WITHOUT DRINKING ALL YOUR BLOOD FIRST. YOU CAN'T ESCAPE US, MCFEARLESS!" They spat out the words and growled some more.

Our father helped us push the desk just far enough for us to gain access to the trapdoor in the floor. He grabbed its latch and lifted it open. The small room was pitch-black, with a ladder leading into what seemed to me an unwelcoming, claustro-phobic black hole. Max and I for sure didn't want to go in there without him. No way!

"Minerva, Max, listen to me! That room is only big enough for the two of you and the Monstra-nomicon. It is protected by every charm the McFear-less family has ever successfully used on a monster. You will be perfectly safe down there. Once you get inside, I'll say the proper magic words to seal you in. Now, listen closely.

After I do that, the door can be opened only from the inside. So no matter what you hear, or think you hear, no matter how badly you want to open that door, do not. Under no circumstances are you to open that door until sunrise tomorrow. The monsters will have to leave under the cover of night. They hate the sun. It burns their evil eyes and fries their fearsome flesh. Do you understand me, children?" We nodded. "Even if it sounds like I'm begging you to do it, do not open that door, not until the sun has come up. Promise me!" commanded our father.

"No, Daddy, please come with us. Don't leave us, please, Daddy, please!" I'm ashamed to say now that I wasn't very brave in that moment of crisis.

BAM! BAM!! BAM!!! BAM!!!! The door wasn't going to hold much longer. Ms. Monstranomicon was screaming her pages out. She was terrified, so my dad scooped her up and handed her to me.

"Promise me," he said again.

"I promise, Dad," said Max.

"No, I won't do it, not without you, Daddy," I begged.

"We don't have time to argue about this, Minerva. Go with the Monstranomi-con down into the monster-proof room now!"

"Okay, fine. I'll do it," I sobbed, and reluctantly did as I was told. I climbed down into darkness, holding my whimpering book friend against my chest.

"Okay, Max. Your turn!" our father said.

Because of Max's swollen hand, my dad had to help him a little. He was halfway down the ladder when my father tried to give him the Bewilder Box.

"Here, Max. I want—" began my father, but he was violently interrupted, and I saw the whole terrible thing.

From directly above him came an eardrum-shattering howl full of rage. The stained-glass dragon window over my father's head exploded and a sea of multicolored glass showered down upon him, lacerating him from head to toe. Then he was struck to the ground by a blow to his head. The Bewilder Box went flying and so did Max, in the opposite direction. Max landed with a thud at my feet, and the Bewilder Box landed somewhere above us. The wind was knocked out of Max when he hit the ground, and his left shoulder was bleeding where pieces of glass had cut him.

When I looked up at the opening of the trap-door, a pair of huge, evil yellow eyes surrounded by matted, lice-ridden, musty fur stared down at me. A dark crusty snout snorted up our scent. Saliva-slathered lips stretched back in a sneer to reveal a set of brown-stained, razor-sharp teeth. I recognized the fiend from the pages of the Monstranomicon. It was the Howleewoof.

"So you're the last of the mighty McFearlesses, and I see that you have that traitor of a monster with you," said the Howleewoof in Monstrosity. "I can't wait to tell my master that she's still alive after all these years. He'll be so delighted to have her back. I'm sure he'll reward me with a nice human hat made from all your uneaten, leftover fleshy bits." The Monstranomicon let out a shriek and cried into my arms, her tears smudging the ink on her pages. I tried to pull the collar of my sweater over my nose to keep from choking on the disgusting stench of the Woof's breath. "How sweet, she likes you—but she's going to miss you. Because once I've finished chomping the legs off your father, I'm going to slow-cook you and your scrawny brother in a giant pot for my creature comrades. They haven't had my children con carne since the last blood moon, and I make it so demonically delicious." Max and I held each other more tightly than we'd ever done before. We didn't want to die such a horrible death. "I'm going to chop you up into tiny chunky pieces of little girl meat and you into little boy—"

The Howleewoof never got to finish its terrifying tirade. My dad clobbered it over the head with his desk chair and then slammed the trapdoor shut on us.

"Remember what I told you: wait for the sun. I love you both dearly," were his final, muffled words. The hole was pitch-black. How would we see the sunrise?

Then our father recited a strange incantation and the door above us clanged as it locked. Max and I tried to figure out what was happening in my father's fiendish fight. We heard the splintering sounds of the barricaded door to my father's study being bashed down, and our hearts sank. It was now four against one. We heard swords clashing

against claws and howls of monster pain. Monster moans, loud bruising bangs from furniture being thrown about and the savage shouts my father gave before attacking all made their way to our terrified ears. Some sounds were clearer than others, but there was no mistaking the final thud of our father's fall. Max, the Monstranomicon and I sobbed and feared the worst when malevolent monster laughter exploded through the sudden silence.

"WE'RE COMING FOR YOU NOW, CHILDREN!" Now that they had finished off my father, they came thundering toward the trapdoor above our cowering heads. But sadly for the monsters, becoming monster food was not our destiny. My father hadn't been wrong about our little hole in the floor. Every inch of it was covered with powerful charms and protective talismans to ward off any evil that might ever try to enter. Each time one of the ferocious fiends tried to touch the trapdoor, its skin caught on fire. Furious howls of searing pain flew from their murdering mouths, and they stomped around in agony.

"OPEN THE DOOR!" They shouted and raged, throwing things into walls and smashing things with their fists.

No matter what they did or tried, we were safe. Our father had made us safe. Max and I hugged each other and waited for a sign of sunlight.

Mr. Devilstone

*T*he trapdoor was open when I woke up. Sunlight poured through the broken stained-glass window and into our monster-proof room. Max groggily woke up, just like I had, and I could tell he was thinking the same things I was: how was the trapdoor opened and who could've opened it? I was totally freaked out. I thought for a second that maybe the monsters had finally broken through our father's last line of defense for us and into our sanctuary. That they were simply waiting until we poked our little heads up, and they'd quickly snap their grisly jaws shut over our skulls and munch us down.

"Max, do you think Dad is okay and maybe he opened the door for us?" I whispered.

"I don't know," Max replied, equally perplexed.

"Let's keep as quiet as we can, just in case, and see if we hear any monster noises above us," I suggested. He nodded, and then we both began to

strain our ears. I detected no movement above us and no sounds of anything at all. Max and I were alone. "There's sunlight coming down here, and Dad did say that sunlight was a monster's burning enemy. So it stands to reason that we're safe, at least for the time being. Don't you think, Max?"

"Yeah, I guess, but how did that door get opened, Mini? I thought Dad said it could only be opened from the inside," said Max, worried.

"He did say that, yes. But if you didn't do it and I didn't do it, then who did?" I wondered aloud.

"It was Dad. It had to have been him. Right, Mini?" Max said. "I mean, who else could possibly have known about this room and how to get the trapdoor open?"

"Well, let's hope so," I said, crossing my fingers. "Daddy? Daddy, are you up there?" I shouted. There was no answer.

"Dad, are you okay? Is it safe for us to come out?" hollered Max.

We called out again and again. But no answers floated back to us. That was when I realized a couple of things that freaked me out even worse than before:

1) The Monstranomicon was missing. I found it highly improbable that she could have opened up that trapdoor, let alone

managed to crawl across the ground and climb up a ladder all by herself.

2) After staring at Max for like a million seconds (well, not really, because that would mean I had to stare at him for 278 hours, and I didn't), I realized that his hand wasn't swollen and he had no cuts or bruises on his body anywhere. And there wasn't even a drop of blood.

What was going on here?

"Why are you looking at me like that, Minerva?" asked Max.

"What did you do, Max?" I said accusingly.

"What do you mean, Minerva? What are you talking about?"

"How is it that you've healed yourself so fast, and where has the Monstranomicon gone?" I demanded.

"Uh . . . I don't know," replied a very nervous Max. "I didn't realize I was all better until you said something about it, Minerva."

"Interesting. What, then, do you think happened in the middle of the night while we both slept?" I stared Max right in the eyes.

"Stop looking at me like that," begged Max. "Minerva, I swear, I don't know. All I remember is

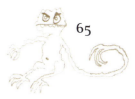

falling off the ladder and hitting the ground. My whole body felt sore and both of my hands were covered in blood. Oh, and I lost the diamond down here somewhere."

"What do you mean you lost the diamond?" I asked, shocked. "You took the strange diamond from the Bewilder Box?"

Max nodded.

"But I saw you put it back inside." Max was even sneakier than I had ever imagined him to be.

"Nope, I swapped it with my trusty marble. I thought the diamond was ten times more amazing, so I borrowed it. When I fell, I dropped it. It's not like it could've gone far in this tiny room. Help me look for it?"

"Rowl."

Before I could answer him and help in the search, an animal-like sound came from above and interrupted us. "Max, what was that?" I said, a little stunned.

"Rowly, rowl," it came again.

"I don't know, but let's check it out," Max said, and pointed at the ladder.

"Grrr, hum!" came the sound once more.

"All right, but let's stay close together," I said, trying to sound as tough as I could. With Max behind me, we cautiously climbed the ladder.

The study was in shambles, and there was no sign of our father or our aggressive attackers from the night before anywhere. It was the biggest mess I'd ever seen. And sitting atop a prominent pile of my father's pulverized possessions was an odd-looking, one-eyed, grayish something-or-other, with a white-tipped tail, wearing a top hat and holding a fancy wooden cane in one of its little clawed paws.

"Look at that, Minerva. My diamond is around that cat's neck," said Max. "Here, kitty-kitty." He tried to coax the animal over to him. No luck. With a roll of its eye, the little critter bared its teeth and growled. "Come on, strange kitty-cat, I won't hurt you. Come here, weirdo kitty-kitty."

"Please don't call me kitty, kitty-cat or weirdo kitty ever again, you little imbecile. I find it insulting, for I am no such thing and so much more than a cat," said the animal with disgust. "Also, the word *kitty* has a rather feline femininity to it, which I feel doesn't describe me in the very least, for I am clearly canine—coyote to be exact—and most assuredly male. And if either of you two dim-witted tiny twits likens me to a cat again, I'll be more than happy to use my *kitty-kitty*-like coyote claws to scratch my way up your legs and past your shoulders, where I'll bite two gaping holes in your necks. Am I understood?"

"Yes, sir," we answered immediately.

"By the way, it took you two bumbling buffoons an eternity to realize that it was safe for you to crawl out of that hole. I despise waiting. However, now that you've arrived, I shall introduce myself. I am Mr. Devilstone, and both of you may call me Mr. Devilstone and *only* Mr. Devilstone. Is that also clear?" said the persnickety one-eyed coyote.

"Yes, sir. It is, sir," we replied, both stunned.

"Nice to meet you, Mr. Devilstone," I said unenthusiastically while I impolitely stared at the eye patch he wore where his other eyeball should have been.

"Um, can I have that diamond back?" asked Max sheepishly.

"Absolutely not, and don't ask me again," Mr. Devilstone said in a way that sent shivers down my spine. "We don't have any more time for this sort of dillydallying, children. Your father has been taken, along with the Bewilder Box. But not all is lost. You see, the monsters wanted what was inside that box, but because it was closed and they didn't have its combination, your father will be kept alive until he reveals it—which is good and bad. Good because he'll be alive, but bad because they'll be bringing him before the king of evil. Once your father is there, the king will want the combination and he'll torture him to get it. I doubt your father will last more than a day or two. So if you want to get him back alive, then we are going to have to act fast."

"How do we know that we can trust you and that you're not working for the monsters while the sun is up?" I asked suspiciously.

"I don't care if you trust me or not, you mindless miniature McFearless," barked Mr. Devilstone. "But if you ever again imply that I work for monsters, I'll scratch out your right eye so that you'll have to wear an eye patch just like the one you've been staring at." I quickly averted my eyes, ashamed that I'd been caught. "Now, let me illuminate some things so that your moronic brains might consider following me into battle. It was I who healed your battered bratty brother by licking his wounds clean after mentioning a few magic words. It was also I who cared for the lovely Ms. Monstranomicon, opened the trapdoor and carried her safely away from the harmful rays of the monster-burning sun. I hazard to think that if I hadn't done so, the two of you McFearless dimwits would still be fumbling around down there in the dark like a pair of sniveling snots until you died of starvation. Now, if we're lucky and if you still want a father, then we might be able to save your beloved Manfred McFearless and, hopefully, the world."

I didn't like the way Mr. Devilstone talked to us one bit. But we were stuck with him, at least for the time being.

Then Mr. Devilstone swung his tail out from behind him. Held within his curled-up tail was a dark green velvet sack that appeared to contain a large square item.

"Hi, Minerva. Hi, Max." The muffled, pleasant, papery voice of the Monstranomicon came from within the sack.

"Are you okay?" I asked, worried about the well-being of my friend.

"Oh, I'm fine," she replied.

"Give her to me, Mr. Devilstone," I begged.

"I'm not going to hurt her, Minervous McFearless," Mr. Devilstone responded snidely.

"You be nice to Minerva, Devilstone," scolded Ms. Monstranomicon protectively. Mr. Devilstone's furry gray face turned embarrassingly crimson for one satisfying second.

"Don't worry about me, Minerva. Mr. Devilstone and I are old friends. He'd never let any harm befall me," she said happily enough. "But that doesn't mean you should let him forget to take me out of here the moment the sun goes down. I'm starting to feel a bit claustrophobic."

I was relieved that Ms. Monstranomicon was okay. But I didn't know if I trusted Mr. Devilstone yet. He did answer a lot of the questions I had, but he left me with a bunch of new ones. Ultimately, I decided that even if this was a trick and he was leading us into the mouths of monsters, it was still probably the best shot we were ever going to have at saving our dad. Max and I were going to have to be smart and keep our wits about us at all times.

"What do you want us to do for you?" I asked.

"Simple. I want you two misbehaving mealworms to help me monsterminate whatever creatures come between us and getting your father back," sighed Mr. Devilstone. "In other words, act like McFearlesses. I've already gone to the trouble of packing up everything I could possibly conceive of that you might need on your first journey into monster battle. So, if we could please now take our leave?" As if by magic, he produced from behind his back a pair of battle-ready satchels, stuffed to capacity with monstermina-tional gear.

Max had a huge smile on his face, from ear to ear. He couldn't wait to go through the satchel, and I'm sure he prayed to his pirate gods that there would be something along the lines of a sword packed inside.

I was still less than thrilled by Mr. Devilstone and his bizarre, aggressive helpfulness. I couldn't quite put my finger on it, but there was something familiar about him that kept pricking annoyingly at my brain. I needed to solve this little mystery soon or I'd go nuts.

I looked at Max, who seemed as ready as he'd ever be for a fight, and he looked at me as if waiting to see what I thought we should do next. Throwing caution to the wind, I picked up my pack and said, "Let's do it. Let's go kick some monster butt and get Dad back!"

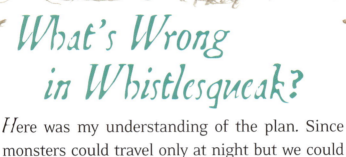

What's Wrong in Whistlesqueak?

*H*ere was my understanding of the plan. Since monsters could travel only at night but we could travel both day and night, the chances of catching up to the creatures that had stolen my father were pretty good. We just had to cover a lot of ground very quickly. Mr. Devilstone's route, based upon the map inside Ms. Monstranomicon's pages, was definitely the fastest one we could possibly take. But it was also the most dangerous. He wanted us to travel west through Whistlesqueak into the overgrown nightmare known as Fangswood Forest; then from there we were somehow to secure ourselves a seaworthy vessel to sail us across the Marshlands of Mold's polluted, bacteria-infested waters. Then we'd head swiftly south through the scalding sands of Skullbury Desert and into the mountainous regions of Zarmevil. Somewhere around there, Mr. Devilstone hypothesized, we'd find our father and hopefully be able to rescue him from the grasp of Castle Doominstinkinfart's evil king.

I know what you're thinking. . . . Sounds like a piece of cake, right? Well, it wasn't.

The monsters had scared off all our horses—or, worse, had eaten them—so we had to set off on our journey on foot. The weight of my satchel was already starting to bother my shoulder and we hadn't even been on the road for more than thirty minutes. Max, who was normally a lazy lump of complaints, seemed totally unaffected by the burden. Mr. Devilstone had us walking at an overly brisk pace, which didn't help my soreness, to say the least. Our cantankerous canine guide was amazingly silent compared to me, with my clomping-around foot-dragging. Max was even louder than me. He banged about like a small tornado filled with exploding bombs and asked stupid questions like "Why are we going this way again?" and "Will someone please buy me some gum balls when we get into town?"

Somewhere along the path, Max had also picked up a fallen branch off the ground and used it to imitate Mr. Devilstone's cane walk. He got away with his rude behavior for a little while, until Mr. Devilstone caught him out of the corner of his only eye, snatched the stick from his hand and smacked him over the head with it three or four times in quick succession. Then he handed it back to Max, who for some reason didn't want it anymore and dropped it. I thought the whole thing was pretty funny, and Max was much quieter after that.

When we finally made it to the center of Whistle-squeak, things just weren't right. It was early after-noon and people should've been busy going from store to store. Families should have been strolling the boulevards in droves, but the town was empty. The signs in some of the shop windows said OPEN, but the doors were locked tightly. It was as if the owners had closed up in a hurry or abandoned their stores to run away from something sinister. The

diamond Mr. Devilstone wore around his neck began to glow bright red. Then an ominous and worried expression appeared on his whiskery face. "Children, I want you to be on guard. There is a monster in our midst. Judging by how brightly my jewel is glowing, I'd say it's not too far from here."

"You mean that diamond lights up when monsters are around? That is the best thing ever, Mr. D!" exclaimed Max.

"Yes, to you it is, Maxwell Monkey Brain," answered Mr. Devilstone insultingly. He then started sniffing the air for clues while his eyeball rapidly darted from left to right and top to bottom, investigating everything he saw on the empty streets. "My senses tell me that the Glorch who helped take your father is here, hiding somewhere in town, and is unfortunately performing more of his monstrously monstrous misconduct."

"Oh, no! What do we do, Mr. Devilstone?" I asked.

"Judging by the faint stink of monster sweat in the air and the pattern of his clawprints, mixed with the other little footprints I've detected, I have regrettably concluded that it has captured all the children of this small town," explained Mr. Devilstone as he pointed to the giant set of monster tracks on the street, as well as the many marks made by feet no bigger than mine. "So, to answer your question,

Minerva, we are going to find that infernal beast, return the uneaten children to their loving parents, gather information as to why your father was taken and then rid this poor town of the Glorch's appalling appetite."

"What's happened to all the grown-ups? Have they been eaten?" I asked, horrified.

"Probably not, Minerva. The grown men and women of this town are all most likely still alive, but nevertheless in danger. Glorches prefer the softer bones of children to chomp. As you might have read, Glorches can spray a toxic mist from the glands above their snouts that renders their prey motionless. It appears this particular Glorch froze the adults so that it could easily kidnap their sons and daughters. The sun is still shining above us, which leaves us only a modicum of time to ready ourselves while the unsuspecting beast slumbers. We are going to have to prepare a potion large enough to unfreeze all the grown-ups and get rid of the Glorch before sundown, or it'll consume all of the children, bite by bite. This is going to be difficult. Let's get started. Open your packs."

"Minerva, this is so exciting,"

Max said. "I'm gonna be a hero, and every time I come back here I'll probably get as much chocolate as I can eat and all the gum balls I can fit in my pockets—all for free. I bet the townsfolk will shout, 'Hurrah, Maxwell McFearless, hurrah!' when I walk the streets. Maybe then I won't have to do as many of the mean things I love doing to you because I'll be too busy being Whistlesqueak's swashbuckling hero."

"Max, I hope Ms. Monstranomicon bites off your pinkie toes next time you fall asleep," I told my dumb brother. "Mr. Devilstone, can you believe what an imbecile my brother is, especially at a time like this?" I couldn't wait for the flood of scathing remarks to fly out of his mouth at Max.

"Actually, I can believe it, and I think you're an imbecile as well," was Mr. Devilstone's disappointing reply. "Now, I want both of you to look inside your satchels for powdered sparrow's beak, essence of squirrel liver, some butterfly milk and peanut butter."

"Yes, sir," I said, a bit upset. I quickly found what he had asked for and then watched him carefully take Ms. Monstranomicon out of her velvet bag in the shade of a shop awning, where she'd be safe from the sun's harmful rays. She had been sleeping and yawned her pages wide open for a deep breath of fresh air.

"Oh my, it's so bright out," complained Ms. Monstranomicon. "Why did you have to wake me up? I was having a wonderful dream that I was nibbling Max's pinkie toes. What's going on?"

"Sorry to have woken you, my darling, but I need to look upon your perfect pages once again. I would like to see—that is, if you don't mind, of course—all the information on the gluttonous Glorch," Mr. Devilstone sweet-talked, kind of making me ill. I looked at Max, and he had an about-to-barf expression on his face.

"Oh . . . umm . . . yes, of course you may. Anything for you, sweetums," she replied, and flipped herself to page 235. (I could have sworn she blushed too.)

❖ THE GLORCH ❖

With an appetite unlike any other, this insatiable breed of monster has the potential to become the largest of our kind. They are normally white, but some have been known to be a light shade of blue. They are virtually invulnerable, with only one known weakness besides their super-sensitivity to the sun: Glorches can never eat the same thing twice. If they consume what they have already once tasted, their bodies shrink to the size they were at birth. Without making gastrointestinal mistakes, these rather unintelligent monsters rapidly expand in size after every unique meal. They can gain up to twelve pounds and grow as much as ten and a half inches in all directions after just one bite. They are hatched from eggs and have to eat their way out to survive. Glorches start to eat immediately, for size is their first line of defense. The second is an immobilizing agent expelled from glands located in their faces, in the form of a fine spray. If the agent is inhaled by humans, its ultimate effect, without treatment, is death. The Glorches' preferred nesting places are dingy basements of old buildings in highly populated areas.

A defensive recipe:
THE FLY MUMMY TOILET BALL

You will need:

- 1 cauldron (or large mixing bowl)
- 1 large wooden spoon
- 1 pair of human hands
- 3 cups of water
- 1 heaping spoonful of peanut butter
- 26 dashes of vinegar (any kind)
- 7 dashes of hot sauce (any kind)
- 1 cup of mayonnaise
- 1 roll of toilet paper
- 1 dead, crusty and dusty fly
- 1 cup of unbleached flour
- 11 minutes of direct sunlight
- 1 timepiece for measuring time

Place the water, the peanut butter, 13 dashes of vinegar, the hot sauce and the mayonnaise into your cauldron or large mixing bowl. Using the large wooden spoon, mix until it's a lumpy, souplike consistency and smells as bad as an iguana's fart. Unroll the toilet paper until it's all a giant, messy pile. Slowly feed the

toilet paper into the cauldron while kneading it with human hands until it becomes a squishy but workable mess. Carefully place the dead, crusty and dusty fly in the center of the mess. Add the remaining 13 dashes of vinegar while checking to see that you haven't lost one of the fly's wings. Using both human hands, form a ball around the fly with the soggy toilet paper. Squish the excess liquid out of the ball to create a nice, firm fly mummy. Roll the fly mummy in flour until it is completely covered. Sniff your fingers; they should smell gross! Take this fly mummy outside and bury it for 11 minutes in direct sunlight. Dig it up and say these magic words to complete the Fly Mummy Toilet Ball:
Glorkeekaydus, gloopahmaydius, shimble, blangle, boof.
Stay away forever, Glorchy, whifflemitten, glinky, poof.
The Fly Mummy Toilet Ball is hated by all Glorches and is sure to ward them off for miles. ⊠

"While I'm making the Glorch antiserum to administer to the frozen adults, I want both of you to make the Fly Mummy Toilet Ball," Mr. Devilstone instructed. "You should have the majority of

the ingredients you'll need inside your packs. For anything else, go across the street to that empty market. Are we clear, Max?"

"Yes, sir," said Max.

"Are we clear, Minerva?" asked Mr. Devilstone.

"Yes, sir," I answered.

"Very good. Take the lovely Ms. Monstranomicon with you just in case your memory is as bad as I think it is, and follow her recipe of defense to the letter. Keep her safely shaded from daylight, even though it is fading fast. Always stick together and stay out of trouble." (I wished he hadn't mentioned the word *trouble*. Fingers crossed that trouble wouldn't come our way.) "I'll meet you all back here in twenty-five minutes. Now go, and don't be late." Mr. Devilstone gently placed Ms. Monstranomicon back in her sack and handed her over to me. (I have to say, I was really happy to have my bundled-up best friend of a book back.)

Max and I quickly discovered that we already had water, a roll of toilet paper, peanut butter, a wooden spoon, a dead, crusty and dusty fly, mayonnaise, vinegar and even a bowl to mix them in. Mr. Devilstone had thought of almost everything. But we were missing the unbleached flour, and we needed to find some kind of hot sauce as well.

"Young Maxwell and Miss Minerva, let's locate those missing ingredients, shall we?" mumbled Ms. Monstranomicon from within her velvet coverings.

"Now that Mr. Devilstone is out of hearing distance," I said with my voice lowered, just in case, "what is going on with you and that grumpy, mean old coyote anyway?"

"Nothing, we're just old friends. Why, did he say something about me while I was asleep?" inquired Ms. Monstranomicon bashfully.

"No, he didn't, but both of you act so weird around each other that I had to ask. Forget I even mentioned it," I said, not entirely believing her. "Let's just go get our missing ingredients so we can get this icky mummy thingy over with already." I strapped my satchel on my shoulder, grabbed Max with my left hand, held Ms. Monstranomicon in my right and started off toward the shadowy market across the street.

The Gluttonous Glorch

*T*he door to the market was unlocked, so we let ourselves in. It was darker than I thought it would be.

Luckily, Max and I had shopped there for groceries with our father a couple of times before, so we had a pretty good idea of the layout of the store.

It got progressively darker and more unpleasant as Max and I crept down the aisles together. Never before in my short life had I seen such a sad and strange phenomenon as the motionless man who blocked our path toward the butcher's bay. He was an elderly Whistlesqueakian gentleman, dressed up in his Sunday best, with a can of sardines clutched in his hand, frozen in midhurl. He never got the chance to throw his canned weapon of choice—the Glorch had gotten to him first. The look on the man's face was the worst part about it for me. His mouth was stuck open like he was in the middle of a terrified scream, and his eyes

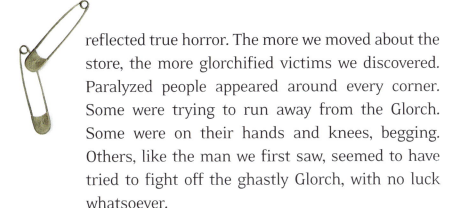

reflected true horror. The more we moved about the store, the more glorchified victims we discovered. Paralyzed people appeared around every corner. Some were trying to run away from the Glorch. Some were on their hands and knees, begging. Others, like the man we first saw, seemed to have tried to fight off the ghastly Glorch, with no luck whatsoever.

"Let's just get what we came here for, make our gross Glorch repellent and get out of here before—"

I didn't get to finish what I wanted to say because—

"Mmhhh! Mmhh! Melp mmus!" came a faint sound.

"What was that? Did you just hear that or am I losing my mind?" I asked Ms. Monstranomicon and Max.

"Yeah, I heard it too. What do you think it is?" asked my brother.

"We need to be on our guard, children," said Ms. Monstranomicon.

"Mmmleeze mmelp mmus," came the desperate noises again. *"Meemore mit mhakes muhp mand mmeats mall muv muss."*

"Max, help me climb atop these shelves so that Ms. Monstranomicon can have a bird's-eye view of the store. Since she can see in the dark, she'll be able to spot something

deadly waiting to jump out at us from the shadows," I suggested quietly. Ms. Monstranomicon agreed that it was an okay plan, while Max, like he always does when he's nervous, snatched a fear-stabilizing gum ball from his pocket, plopped it in his mouth, chewed it vigorously and nodded.

"Miz menee mawdee mare?" came the sounds even more frantically.

"It doesn't sound like one of my monstrous relatives, but be careful anyway. It might be a trap," reported Ms. Monstranomicon as Max helped me quietly climb up the shelves, secure a position for Ms. Monstranomicon high atop a large jar of saltwater string beans and climb back down again.

Max decided he didn't like the thought of walking into a potential trap without a weapon, so he searched his satchel. He found his old slingshot with *Maximillius* etched into its handle, which surprised him, since he hadn't seen or used it in a long time. He was quite good with the miniature Y-shaped catapult contraption—and he should have been, considering that the last time he'd had it he'd intentionally shot out most of our neighbor's windows before my father confiscated it. I could tell it felt good to Max to have his old trusted slingshot back in action, and it increased his much-needed monster-fighting confidence.

He tested the elastic part of the sling a couple of times by pulling it back to his elbow, holding it in firing position and releasing it with a snap. "Seems to be in tip-top shape, but I should test out my aim real quick just to make sure I still have what it takes," Max said, and reached into his pocket once again for a gum ball. In one swift, fluid movement, Max placed the sour-apple-flavored munchable monster munition into the sling, took aim at a bottle of ground nutmeg fifty feet away and fired before the words "Max, that's a *really* bad idea" could escape my mouth.

The gum ball blasted the nutmeg right off the shelf, knocking it effortlessly and inconveniently into similar breakable bottles and causing a domino effect that led to a very loud *crash!* The floor began to vibrate intensely. Something growled and started burrowing its way up from the bowels of the market. Something humongous. Suddenly, the Glorch exploded through the floorboards just a few feet away from where we stood. I'd never seen such a huge living thing in all my life. My father had once taken Max and me to see the elephants at the zoo, and the Glorch must have been at least three times their size—and three times more frightening. Its fat face was reptilian, and it walked about on four enormous clawed feet. Having to support such a massive stomach had flattened them out—and transformed its blubbery legs into powerfully muscled limbs capable of kicking a man in half.

Ms. Monstranomicon screamed, "*Help meeeeeeee, Minerva!*" so loudly, my eardrums almost burst. One of the Glorch's huge, yellowy white, pudgy claws had grabbed her and was scratching the sensitive skin of her cover with its dirty nails.

That was when I discovered what had been making those strange noises. Held in the Glorch's other fat claw was a long rusty iron chain—and all of Whistlesqueak's missing children were con-

nected to it with collars. It was their muffled pleas for help that we'd been hearing from below, where they were hidden down in the Glorch's underground lair. Tears of hopelessness poured down their miserable, dirty faces from their soggy red eyes. They were all beyond terrified. The Glorch had chained them up so that none of them would be able to escape during its sunlight-avoiding snooze. It was a shockingly sad thing to see. It made Max and me McFearlessly mad—no, scratch that. It made us monsterminatingly mad. We *had* to do something.

A Glorchtastic Plan

*I*n the chaos, Max and I had a small window of opportunity to quickly flesh out a plan to rescue our fellow Whistlesqueakians. Max rushed off to do his part while I stayed to confront the beast.

"GNNAHHNN, GNNAHRRR!" the Glorch groaned, scanning the area around it with giant overdeveloped eyes that rolled around in its pre-historic head. It looked like a gargantuanly over-weight salamander with crooked horns hanging over its bloated monster face. "I HATE IT WHEN MY TUMMY AND ME ARE SO RUDELY WOKEN UP LIKE THIS. BUT I IMAGINE THAT THE EAT-ING OF TWO MINIATURE MIGHTY MCFEAR-LESSES FIRST THING AFTER A LESS-THAN-GLORCHERRIFIC NAP WOULD MAKE US FEEL A LOT BETTER, DON'T YOU THINK SO, BELLY?" the Glorch roared while rubbing its enormous, hungry stomach.

"I'm sorry about your nap, Mr. Glorch, but it

wasn't my fault," I said, speaking to it in its own (forbidden for humans to use) native tongue, Monstrosity. "You see, Max had an accident with a gum ball and some nutmeg. I promise it won't happen again. I have an idea, though, about how we might be able to make it up to you. How about you release the children and give me back my book best friend and then we'll all walk out of here like nothing ever happened? Then, if you want, Max and I will come back here and help you get back to sleep—permanently." It was obviously confused by my being able to communicate with it like a fellow monster would have, and I could tell that my boldness unnerved it. My strategy was to stall the Glorch from eating me until Max was ready with the second phase of our monsterminating plan.

"DON'T BE SILLY, YOU MOST DEFINITELY GOOD-TASTING, WRONG-IDEA'D LITTLE MCFEARLESS MORSEL. I ABSOLUTELY WILL NOT DO ANYTHING OF THE SORT. MY TERRIBLE TUMMY COULDN'T ALLOW SUCH A STARVING THING LIKE THAT TO HAPPEN TO ME, AND YOU MUST BE INSANE IF YOU THINK A LITTLE GIRL LIKE YOU STANDS A CHANCE AGAINST A MAGNIFICENT MONSTER SUCH AS ME." The Glorch took deep sucks of air through its nasty snot-dripping nostrils, which flexed open and closed like gills on a hammerhead shark. "I WONDER, WHERE HAS

YOUR CHICKEN OF A BROTHER RUN OFF TO, HUH? HE MUST BE THE SANE SIBLING, HIDING AND TREMBLING SOMEWHERE IN A CORNER. I CAN SMELL THAT HE'S STILL AROUND HERE AND I CAN HARDLY WAIT TO FIND HIM. OH, HOW I LOVE A FINELY PREPARED BITE OF LEG OF LITTLE BROTHER WITH HIS SISTER WATCHING IN HORROR AS I EAT HIM. IT'S ONE OF MY FAVORITE MONSTER MEALS."

"I wouldn't worry yourself about Max, Mr. Glorch. I'd worry more about your decision not to let everyone go. It really is a shame you feel that way, and I'm afraid that I simply can't allow you to harm anyone else here in Whistlesqueak." My lack of reaction to its threats confused the Glorch thoroughly. It was having a hard time figuring out what it should do about me. (Eating me was an option I wouldn't like.) "You wouldn't happen to have a first name, by any chance, would you? I want to make sure I know what the first name of the first monster Max and I properly monsterminate is," I said, keeping up my charade.

"THIS IS PURE POPPYCOCK, AND YES, I DO HAVE A FIRST NAME. IT'S GREBLOR, GREBLOR GLORCH. NOW, WHY AREN'T YOU SCARED OF ME? YOU REALLY ARE SUPPOSED TO BE SCARED OF ME. WHAT IS WRONG WITH YOU?" asked Greblor, suspicious and enraged.

"You're joking, right? You're not scary at all," I lied. "You seem like you're a really sweet monster. But now you've done a bunch of bad things and it's time that you were punished." The Glorch didn't like that answer, not one bit.

"ARE YOU OUT OF YOUR MCFEARLESS MIND, CHILD? ONLY A FOOL WOULD TALK TO ME LIKE YOU'RE DOING," answered Greblor angrily. "I'VE ALWAYS BEEN THE MOST UNSWEETENED, DOWNRIGHT SALTY MONSTER ANYONE HAS EVER LAID EYES ON. NOW, I'M STARVING AND YOU'RE REALLY GETTING ON MY NERVES. I HAVE TO EAT YOU RIGHT AWAY."

Greblor lunged, openmouthed, toward me and tried to snap his jaws around my waist, but I was too fast for his fat body to catch.

"Well, that wasn't nice," I said.

"PLEASE JUST SHUT YOUR TASTY FACE UP AND LET ME EAT YOU. I'M SICK OF ALL YOUR SILLY LITTLE STATEMENTS, AND IF I HAVE TO HEAR ANY MORE OF THEM, I'M GOING TO THROW UP ALL THE DIFFERENT PEOPLE I'VE ALREADY EATEN HERE IN TOWN. AND THROW-ING UP IS SUCH A HUGE DISAPPOINTMENT TO ME. I'VE ALWAYS HATED DOING IT. NOT BECAUSE I DON'T WANT TO EAT MY OWN BARF BACK UP OFF THE GROUND. I DO, AND I LOVE EATING OTHER PEOPLE'S BARF LIKE THAT. IT'S

BECAUSE I CAN'T RE-EAT MY OWN VOMIT ONCE I'VE BARFED IT OUT OF ME THAT MAKES ME HATE THROWING UP SO MUCH. IT'S JUST SUCH A SHAME, DON'T YOU THINK?" asked the gross Glorch, and he tried to chomp me again.

"Yeah, if you say so," I said, dodging him for the second time. Listening to him talk about puking made me want to puke, and the thought of him eating my puke made me want to puke even harder. Max had to hurry, because eventually Greblor Glorch might get lucky and swallow me up. He was getting closer with every try. "Hey, are there other monsters here in town too, or are you the only monster Max and I will be monsterminating in Whistlesqueak?" I asked, ducking out of the way of another jaw-snap.

"NO, THEY'RE LONG GONE WITH YOUR FATHER BY NOW. I ONLY STUCK AROUND HERE SO THAT I COULD CHOMP UP ALL THE CHILDREN THIS TOWN HAD TO OFFER. STOP MOVING AROUND SO MUCH, MCFEARLESS," said the Glorch, out of breath. "NOW, I'M WILLING TO MAKE A DEAL WITH YOU. IF YOU PROMISE TO WALK DIRECTLY INTO MY MOUTH WITHOUT A FUSS, I SWEAR I'LL SAVOR EVERY LAST NUTRITIOUS PART OF YOU WHILE I COLDHEARTEDLY CHEW YOU UP. BUT IF YOU KEEP MAKING ME EXERCISE, THEN I'LL BE FORCED TO FEED YOU TO

MYSELF AS PAINFULLY AS MY STOMACH CAN POSSIBLY ALLOW," growled the Glorch, and he lunged toward me once again, too close for comfort.

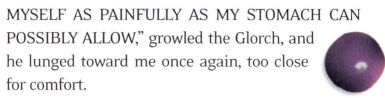

That was when Max reappeared, slingshot in hand. He pulled it back and slung a perfectly placed grape-flavored purple gum ball right down the Glorch's throat.

"MMMM, GRAPE. APPETIZERS BEFORE I EAT THE MAIN COURSE? I LIKE THE WAY YOU BOTH THINK. NEVER HAD ONE OF THOSE BEFORE, BUT I CAN'T LET YOU DO THAT AGAIN," the Glorch said, and slammed his tail down as hard as he could. The whole room shook like an earthquake, and I almost fell over. Max was caught off balance and fell to the floor, spilling the only handful of grape gum balls he had. He didn't have two of any other flavor left in his pocket gum ball artillery (since the grape ones are his least favorite to chew, they're always the last ones to go), so he needed to get at least one of them back to be able to poison the Glorch.

"YOU NAUGHTY MCFEARLESS MEAT PUP-PETS WILL SLIP UP SOON, AND I'LL BE THERE TO RIP YOU TO SHREDS," screamed the world's most frustrated Glorch. He thrashed about, knocking over everything in the store with his hulking frame, mindless of the damage he was causing. The chains connected to the poor children were pulled in every direction. Things were getting out of control.

Max barely rolled out of the way of one of the Glorch's tail swipes, his head almost crunched by its crushing blow. Poor Max was having trouble keeping track of the rolling purple gum balls that we desperately needed. Every time he'd almost get his hands on a precious purple piece of chewy good-ness, Greblor would stop him, or it would roll too dangerously close to the Glorch's rampaging feet for Max to snatch it back safely. There were four purple shots of gum left. Unfortunately, Greblor stepped on and destroyed three of them, which left us with only

one shot, and that was only if we could get to it before it too was destroyed. Both Max and I spotted the last remaining gum ball as it rolled through the Glorch's legs and into a corner. It was now or never. I had to create a diversion so that Max could get to it and then get it down Greblor's evil throat or we were all dead meat.

"Hey, tubby! Over here, slowpoke," I called, insulting him in my most condescending voice. "You're an embarrassment to all monsterkind. It must be driving you insane that an eleven-year-old girl is too fast for your fat body to catch."

"ARRGGHHHH, THAT IS IT! YOU'RE DEAD!" growled one very fed-up Glorch.

I must have said something right, because Greblor brought his full attention back to me. Hopefully, Max would have all the time he needed to get his gum ball. The Glorch charged at me, head down, like a battering ram, with the chains full of children in tow. This time he was too fast. One of the many horns that adorned his creature cranium connected with my shoulder blade, sending me flying into the air like a rag doll. I landed hard and I was hurt. I was hurt bad. I started to weep, which Greblor loved.

"DO I HEAR CRYING? OH, HOW THOUGHTFUL OF YOU," he said, satisfied. "YOU DIDN'T HAVE TO GO TO THE TROUBLE OF MAKING ALL THAT EYE SAUCE TO ACCOMPANY YOUR FACE FOR WHEN I

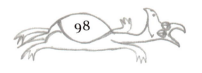

EAT IT OFF, MINERVA. I'M SURE MY TUMMY AND I WOULD FIND YOU DELICIOUS SIMPLY PLAIN."

The floor rumbled again. The Glorch started to charge once more, this time bearing down on me with his jaws wide open for the kill. Searching for something to defend myself with, I found a hammer on the ground. With all my might, I threw it at Greblor's face. Although it never even touched him, a glorchtastically great thing happened. Greblor ducked away from my tossed hammer and accidentally jammed his biggest monster toe into the store's stone wall. He banged it so hard that his big toenail bent back and broke off in a fountain of bloody toe gore.

"OH! OW! OW! OW! MY TOE! YOU WORTHLESS, WRETCHED CHILD, SEE WHAT YOU MADE ME DO! WHEN I GET MY CLAWS AROUND YOU, I'M GOING TO COMPRESS YOUR HEAD INTO YOUR FEET, BREAK YOUR SPINE INTO A MILLION PIECES AND PLAY YOU LIKE AN ACCORDION. OW, MY POOR HUNGRY TOE!" He howled in unbearable agony and hopped around in circles.

"Mini, are you okay?" asked Max, appearing by my side.

"I'm hurt pretty bad, but I'll manage," I replied. "Did you get it?"

"Yeah, Mini, I got it," he said, staring at my wound.

"Then forget about me, Max. Just send that monster back to whatever monster hole it came from!" I cried between whimpers.

"Hey, Glorchy! This is for my sister!" Max shouted to the ghastly Glorch—and fired.

Everything moved in slow motion. Max and I both stared at the trajectory of the purple gum ball and prayed. The Glorch's face contorted from a look of pain to one of sheer terror when he realized what was speeding toward his mouth. The Glorch was in the middle of an openmouthed toe moan, while the doom-infused purple gum ball of Glorch destruction was inches away from his face. My heart was pounding. I could feel every beat throughout my body. Time stood still. Max truly was a great shot, and the Glorch was finally going to get what he deserved. The gum ball found its mark—but not the one we needed. I heard the *tink* it made when it hit one of Greblor's razor-sharp teeth and ricocheted harmlessly to the floor, where Greblor stepped on it.

We were going to die.

"POOR LITTLE MAX AND HIS ANNOYING SISTER, MINERVA. WHERE HAS ALL YOUR HOPE GONE? YOU HAVE NOTHING LEFT." His words rang true. I believed in that final moment that we were doomed. Max, however, did not. He raised his slingshot one more time and

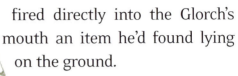

fired directly into the Glorch's mouth an item he'd found lying on the ground.

"WHAT DELICIOUS ITEM HAVE YOU MADE ME SWAL-LOW NOW?" the Glorch asked Max, not worried in the least. "I RATHER ENJOYED THAT. IT HAD A HARD, SLIMY OUTSIDE THAT WAS SALTY AND AN ALMOST CRUNCHY, CHEESY, DECOMPOSING ELEMENT TO IT THAT I FOUND TO BE EXTRAORDINARY. IT WAS MAYBE THE BEST THING THAT I'VE EVER TASTED, YET SOMEHOW FAMILIAR. YOU MUST TELL ME BEFORE YOU BOTH DIE IN MY MOUTH, WHAT WAS IT?"

I looked at my brother, because I also had no idea.

"That was your disgusting toenail. You ate your-self," Max said with a smile.

And the once confident stare of our enemy disappeared altogether.

"YOU'VE POISONED ME! I'VE BEEN POI-SONED BY TWO STUPID LITTLE KIDS. HOW CAN THIS BE?" moaned Greblor. "ALL THE THINGS I'VE HAD TO EAT OVER THE YEARS TO GET TO THIS SIZE—IT'LL TAKE ME FOREVER TO DO THAT AGAIN. THIS CAN'T BE HAPPENING TO ME." The impressively huge Glorch rapidly started to shrink.

Within moments, Greblor was the size of a baby frog.

(It was brilliant on Max's part, really. You see, since a Glorch eats its way out of its own shell when hatching, it makes perfect sense that if it ate a part of itself later in life, the results would be detrimental.)

"Well done, children," said Mr. Devilstone from out of nowhere. He picked up the helplessly tiny Greblor, put him in his mouth and swallowed him.

"Ewww, that was so gross!" I said woozily, and fell over. . . .

Strange Visions and Bumpy Roads

*W*hile I lay bleeding on the ground, going in and out of consciousness, Mr. Devilstone, Max and Ms. Monstranomicon went about helping the town. They unfroze the adults with Mr. Devilstone's Glorch antivenin. Then they released all the children, tended to their wounds and reunited them with their incredibly grateful parents.

Max was heralded for his courage and rewarded with free gum balls for life (just like he'd wanted, and he greedily stuffed his pockets full of them) as Whistlesqueak's very own "brave and mighty monster slayer." Which made me so mad. It was like they thought I had nothing to do with saving any of them at all. Maybe it was because I was badly injured and I could barely stay awake that all of the heroic focus went to "The Mighty Maxwell McFearless," who lives just up the road with "that poor injured girl over there." Forget the fact that I'm his older sister and I was practically impaled while trying to save everybody. All I heard anyone say as I painfully awaited medical attention was "Oh, it's that weird McFearless girl. Looks to me like she's not going to make it," and "I hate to say this, but I'm glad it's not my daughter lying there." You'd think someone would at least have called me brave too. But no, no one did.

Max and Ms. Monstranomicon happily showed the townsfolk how to make some of her defensive recipes, in case of future monster attacks. They were obliged once again and showered Max with tasty treats and many more thank-yous (none for Minerva). While I sat unnoticed and in pain, watching the adoration that unfolded around Max, I realized that I didn't need the townsfolk's gratitude or accolades. I just wanted help. Eventually, after everyone else in town was tended to, Mr. Devilstone came to my aid. He scooped me into his furry coyote arms; then he placed me gently into the back of an old horse-drawn cart.

"You were incredibly brave back there, and I'm proud of the way you handled yourself," he said, and then apologized for having taken such a long time to tend to me. He explained that he'd needed to make a powerful and complicated potion that could heal my wounds rapidly.

"Now, I know that you are in a lot of pain, but I need to warn you that this

potion can have strange side effects that will not be to your liking," he said in a stern but caring voice.

"Yeah, okay," I said, just wanting the pain in my shoulder to stop.

"All right, tilt your head back and open your mouth." Mr. Devilstone unscrewed the shiny silver top half of his cane's handle, revealing a hidden compartment. He turned the cane over and a tiny blue bottle with a tiny blue cork plopped out.

Then, without wasting any more time, he pulled out the cork and poured the potion down my throat.

It was the worst thing I'd ever tasted in my whole entire life. Once the potion hit my stomach, things only got worse. It felt like a fire had been set in the back of my throat, and I was sure that my tongue had melted away. After a few moments, my mouth finally calmed down to a somewhat normal state. In fact, the only bad side effect from the potion—besides its temporarily turning my teeth fluorescent blue, the gross aftertaste and the clumps of itchy hair that sprouted on my tongue—was Max's face as he laughed at my discomfort. I swore to myself that the moment my shoulder healed, I was going to strangle him.

"Yuck, what was in that stuff?" I asked, noticing that my shoulder had rapidly started to feel much better.

"Some skunk-liver oil, chopped moose bladder,

the droppings from a—" began Mr. Devilstone, but I had to shut him up. There are certain things a girl my age just doesn't need to know.

"Now, try to take it easy, lie down and let the potion do the rest of its work," said Mr. Devilstone, reassembling his cane.

I listened to Mr. Devilstone, shot Max an evil stare and tried my best to get as comfortable as I could. We'd lost precious time in Whistlesqueak and we needed to get back on the road quickly if we were ever going to stand a chance at catching up with my father. The grateful townsfolk had provided us with water, food and blankets, along with their fastest horses to pull the cart.

Mr. Devilstone cracked the horses' reins and hurried us all along toward the very frightening Fangswood Forest.

The potion's power was amazing. Its magic had gone to work, repairing the deep wound on my shoulder. It felt as if I had hundreds of army ants rebuilding me so that I might McFearlessly fight once again. The potion, however, could do nothing to help with the way Mr. Devilstone was driving. He really wanted to make up for lost time, so he drove the horses hard, whipping them until we were traveling as fast as their legs could possibly carry us through twisty turns and over butt-breaking road bumps.

While I lay there under the starry night sky with my head bouncing brutally around on my neck, I closed my eyes for just a second. Strange visions appeared in my mind, perhaps just more of the potion's strange side effects that Mr. Devilstone had warned me about.

It was as if I had been teleported to an evil underground cavern, where I was an invisible fly on the wall. My poor father was tied to a chair and there were two monsters tormenting him. One of them was a Swoggler, a nasty caterpillar-like monster with a sickeningly massive saber-toothed sucker mouth and several snakelike sucker tentacles.

✦ THE SWOGGLER ✦

These sickly white, caterpillar-like memory vampires are a particularly vile species. Swogglers' only food source is the memories and emotions found inside the brains of their victims. They possess giant saber-toothed sucker mouths filled with multiple rows of razor-sharp needle teeth that aid them greatly during mind feedings. Swogglers have six long suction-cupping tentacles to hold their prey steady, and they can expand their oral cavities up to seven times their normal size to accommodate the wide variety of skulls found in nature. No human head or animal cranium is too big for these experience-leeching memory monsters to feast upon. More often than not, swoggled victims are left as mindless empty shells of their former selves. Though blind, Swogglers navigate easily by use of their hyperrealized senses of smell and taste, making them the perfect hunters in the dark. Swogglers produce copious amounts of saliva and can spit very thick globules of it at intended targets with pinpoint accuracy. The creatures often use this tactic to stun or blind their victims just long enough for them to attack or to escape. Swogglers hate the cold and prefer small heated spaces in which to live. Some older Swogglers have been known to develop unique evil abilities that make them far more dangerous than their younger counterparts. All Swogglers are well known for deceit and treachery and should never be trusted under *any* circumstances.

A defensive recipe:

FROZEN MUSTARD SOUP

✦•◦•◦•◦•◦•✦•◦•◦•◦•✦•◦•◦•◦•◦•✦•◦•◦•◦•◦•✦•◦•◦•✦

You will need:

- 1 cauldron (or large mixing bowl)
- 1 large silver fork
- 1 voice for barking with
- 1 pair of human hands
- 1 hard-boiled egg
- 1 teaspoon of house dust
- 2 strands of hair from your own head
- 1 cup of mustard
- 3 dead ants
- 2 cups of ice
- 13 strands of dog hair (the dirtier and smellier the better)
- 1 timepiece for measuring time

Place the hard-boiled egg (shell and all), house dust and strands of hair from your own head into your cauldron or large mixing bowl and blend together, stirring everything counterclockwise with the large silver fork for one minute. Next, bark like a dog 5 times as loudly as you can. Then add the mustard, dead ants and ice and slowly stir the entire mixture clockwise for another minute or until lumpy. Once lumps have formed, begin to add the strands of dog hair. Bark once, as loudly as possible, after each strand is added. (You will be using 13 strands of dog hair, which means you must bark 13 times.) With human hands, squish everything together and say these magic words: *Poo, poopy, swog, swoggle, brain licker, poop. Rain slicker, watermelon, frozen mustard soup.* Wipe your dirty hands on the closest clean wall and place your cauldron in the coldest place you can find in your house. Leave it there overnight so that an invisible protective stink barrier will form around your dwelling. Swogglers will immediately catch a cold if any part of the Frozen Mustard Soup so much as even touches them and will die if they ever ingest it. Frozen Mustard Soup will keep you safe from a Swoggler's brain-sucking for 7 months. Ⓜ

The hideous monster beside the Swoggler was an evil creature (my hands are shaking as I write this) I'd never seen inside the pages of the Monstranomicon. A huge, hulking, twelve-hundred-pound gargoyle, who with a whisper of its demonically ice-cold voice could make plants wither and give cats nosebleeds. It had opaque, unblinking, sharklike eyes, a bat snout for a nose and a mouthful of fearsome fangs. A long, forked serpent tongue darted out periodically to lick its slippery, moist, eelskin-looking lips. It had a monstrously muscular body covered in patches of prickly hair and dragon scales of varying shades of black. Its two talon-clawed hands were clenched into fists, and a set of vampire wings were closely folded against its back. Basically, it was the scariest monster ever.

"Tell me the combination to the Bewilder Box and I'll set you free to see your children once again," it lied.

"Never, beast!" shouted my father.

"I only offer to save you from the pain, Manfred. My Swoggler slave can easily extract everything I need directly from your brain—but you'll be in agony. Every suck he takes will steal more and more of your memories, until you have nothing left. And I doubt that you want that, Manfred McFearless, son of Milton, who was the son of Martin, who was the son of Mandrake, whose father was my mortal enemy, Maximillius McFearless. So please, just tell me what I want to know

before I lose my temper and kill you by accident," said the scariest monster ever through gritted fangs.

"I am a McFearless and I'll *never* give in to your trickery, beast!" My father spat directly into the creature's face. That wasn't the best idea—the ramifications were severe. The horned beast began to beat my father with its cruel claws.

I wanted nothing more than to wake myself from this nightmarish vision, but I couldn't. I was trapped. Just like my father—trapped.

Then, with a snap of its fingers, the fiend signaled for its Swoggler and let it loose upon my father's mind.

"SSssyesSS, SSssmaster, SSssthank SSssyou, SSssmaster," said the Swoggler, drooling.

Why couldn't I wake up? I didn't want to see this.

The Swoggler opened its saber-toothed sucker mouth wide to reveal thousands of tiny serrated needle teeth. Saliva dripped down my father's face from the Swoggler's constricting lips as it positioned its wormy mouth around his head, creating the suctioning seal necessary to extract the nourishing information its master wanted—and its own tummy craved. My father's scream was horrifying (the memory of it haunts me still) and marked the first time I had ever seen tears fall from his eyes.

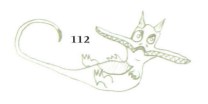

Both monsters found this hilarious and savored his agony.

"SSsslet SSssme SSssin SSssto SSssyour SSsshead, SSssMcFearlessSS," hissed the Swoggler. "SSssmy SSssmaster SSsswantsSS SSssthe SSsscombination."

My father tried as hard as he could not to answer the inquisitorial demands of the beast, but nothing was safe from the Swoggler's giant, leeching mouth. It feasted from a fountain full of my father's first McFearless memories and stole precious moments he held hidden in his heart. It was futile for my father to resist. The Swoggler savagely

sucked and sucked until the answer it needed came easily out of my father's head.

"You may stop now, slave. I may need something more from him later," said the hateful shark-eyed creature. "I'm afraid you may already have ruined him."

"SSssyesSS, SSsssmaster, SSsssasSS SSssyou SSsswish," the Swoggler said obediently, and released my barely breathing father from its mouth.

Now that the gargoyle monster finally had the combination to the Bewilder Box, nothing could stop it. Its giant fingers worked the tricky patterns and grooves until the box was open. But what should have been a victorious sharp-toothed smile was instead an ice-cold deadly frown. "Where is it, Manfred?" shrieked the beast with terrible fury, crushing a useless marble between its long, powerful fingers.

When my father realized what his mischievous son had done, a faint smile came to his face. "Max," he whispered to himself. Then his heart stopped beating.

"No!" I screamed wildly, bolting awake with my heart pounding and my body drenched in sweat. Max was so shocked by my outburst that he flung his arms about and unfortunately knocked the reins of our horse-drawn cart right out of Mr. Devilstone's paws.

"Nice work, Max," said the coyote unhappily, holding on to his top hat while he fished for the fallen reins. To make matters worse, the diamond around Mr. Devilstone's neck began to glow, and the horses became spooked by something, no doubt evil, hiding in the woods. They whinnied and reared up on their hind legs, violently kicking into the night air. Under no one's control, the horses began to pick up speed and zigzagged in a panicked frenzy.

"Do something!" shouted Ms. Monstranomicon desperately, opening and slamming her cover with each syllable. Max held on to the front railing while he tried his best to grab hold of Ms. Monstranomicon. The cart wildly jolted up and down, and I was launched into the air. I tumbled head over heels across the damp earth and through the tall grass of Fangswood Forest. Eventually, I came to a hard stop and watched the others speed off uncontrollably down the road without me.

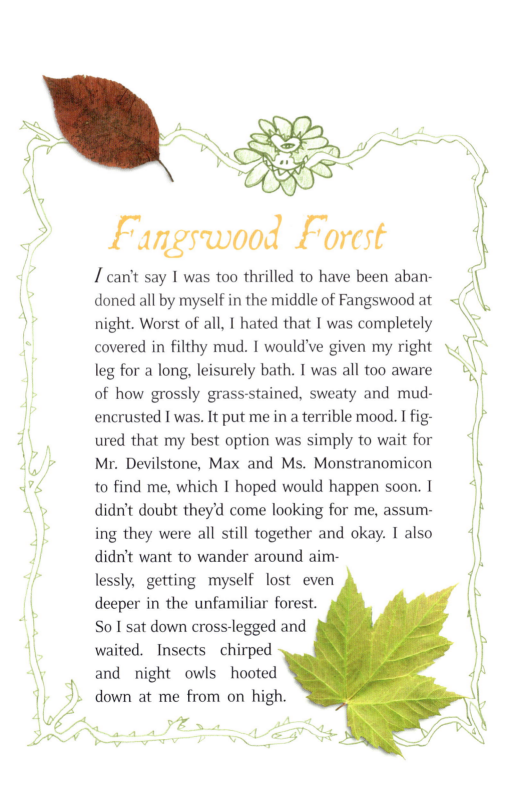

Fangswood Forest

I can't say I was too thrilled to have been abandoned all by myself in the middle of Fangswood at night. Worst of all, I hated that I was completely covered in filthy mud. I would've given my right leg for a long, leisurely bath. I was all too aware of how grossly grass-stained, sweaty and mud-encrusted I was. It put me in a terrible mood. I figured that my best option was simply to wait for Mr. Devilstone, Max and Ms. Monstranomicon to find me, which I hoped would happen soon. I didn't doubt they'd come looking for me, assuming they were all still together and okay. I also didn't want to wander around aimlessly, getting myself lost even deeper in the unfamiliar forest. So I sat down cross-legged and waited. Insects chirped and night owls hooted down at me from on high.

Thousand-year-old trees loomed eerily above me. Their trunks had grown so tremendously thick over time that the distance between them was only inches. Some had even grown into one another and cast horrifyingly twisted shadow shapes across the ground.

Finding Max's satchel, not too far away from me, barely brightened my spirits. It had somehow followed me off the cart and wound up wedged in a jagged stump. Once I had the pack in my hands, I pulled out one of Max's clean shirts and happily used it to wipe away as much of the muddy dirt as I could, hopefully leaving a permanent stain. Now, *that* made me feel a whole lot better. I also found a few large strips of peppered buffalo jerky, which I hungrily put in my mouth.

Time passed without any sign of Max, Mr. Devilstone or Ms. Monstranomicon, and the forest seemed to grow darker and more sinister while I waited. And it also made me nervous. In the quiet of the darkness, my heartbeat was the only thing that kept me company. That was when I noticed that there were no more bugs chirping and the night birds no longer hooted at the moon. Everything had suddenly grown deathly still, and a distinctively bad feeling that I was being watched crept over me.

"Owahroooo ow ow owrooo!" I heard the guttural howl of an

unknown creature coming from somewhere behind me.

The savage wailing cry conveyed hunger and a thirst for blood. I spun around to see if I could catch a glimpse of whatever was making the noise, but it was too dark.

"Owrooo, I'm coming for you!" Another snarling howl came, closer than the last.

It was very unsettling. I moved around in slow circles with my guard up, waiting for whatever was stalking me to show itself.

"I've missed you, McFearless," whispered a scratchy animal-like voice, even closer still, reverberating off the trees in all directions. Whoever or whatever was doing this enjoyed toying with me and was trying to scare me out of my mind before it attacked. Guess what? It was working.

"Here I come, Minerva," threatened the mystery monster voice.

I had very little time before the monster came for me; I was sure of that. If I was going to stand a fighting chance, I needed a weapon. I dove for Max's satchel just as the sound of fallen leaves being crunched by quickly running monster feet caught my attention. Before I reached the pack, I was yanked upside down by my ankles.

"Owahrooo! Not a chance, my little meaty

morsel. Who knows what kinds of danger you might have stored in there?" said the all-too-familiar voice of the Howleewoof.

My face turned red as all my blood suddenly rushed down toward my head. The Woof's viselike monster hands tightly held me suspended in the air while I pounded on its thick, hairy, mangy coat with my bare fists.

"Hello, McFearless. Have you missed me since my last uninvited visit? I know I missed you—missed not *eating* you, that is." The Howleewoof exhaled putrid bursts of hot stink into my face through its fangs. The odor burnt my eyes as if I had been cutting thousands of raw onions inches away from my eyelids.

"Put me down!" I screamed, writhing within its grip. "And where is my father? What have you done with him, you fiend?"

"How about no? And in answer to your second and third questions, boo-hoo for you, my master's got him," barked the Woof condescendingly, without taking its huge, unblinking yellow eyes off me. "He just couldn't wait any longer to get at what was in your father's Bewilder Box, so he flew all the way down here, snatched him up and took him back to Doominstinkinfart to torture—which means, sadly for you, that your daddy has probably already gone bye-bye. Sorry, my little snack!" The news of my father scared me and made me think that the vision I'd had of him earlier wasn't just a dream. *No, I thought, it couldn't have been real.* But my father needed me, and I needed to escape.

"If you value your life, monster, then you'll let me go, because my friends will be here any second with some reinforcements from Whistlesqueak!" I lied, trying to scare the Howleewoof.

"Would these be the same people whose horses I spooked, which led to me having you here? The same ones who won't be able to hear your screams while I'm eating you?" said the Howleewoof mockingly as droplets of its spittle landed on my cheek. "Your lies don't scare me, Minerva. And for your information, I highly doubt that anyone will be leaving Whistlesqueak or living there ever again. You see, my gargantuan friend Greblor is there right now as we speak and is probably finishing off the last of the Whistlesqueakians as I'm saying this,

having tracked down anyone dumb enough to stay in town." The stench of the Woof's hot, fetid breath made me gag.

"You are in serious need of a mint, did you know that?" I said, secretly eyeballing Max's satchel.

"What are you talking about? My breath is fantastic," said the Woof, intentionally blowing its hot, stinky breath directly at my nose. "All the lady Woofs love it." It was torture.

"No, your breath is absolutely killing me—kind of like the way Max and I killed your fat friend Greblor," I said, moving my head back and forth in search of spots of fresh air, trying desperately not to smell the beast's bad breath.

"Spare me your tall tales, little liar," the Howleewoof snarled. "Like I said, I'm sure Greblor's eaten up everybody in Whistlesqueak by now and grown even more monolithically monstrous in the process. You could never have stopped him and his insidious appetite. Even I get scared of him sometimes."

"No, it's true." I gasped the words while I fought to keep myself from gagging. "We tricked him into eating himself, and when he shrank to a bite-sized coyote chomp, our friend ate him up. Now, I'm begging you, please let me go. Haven't you ever heard of brushing your teeth?"

"How dare you keep making up those impossible fibs about one of my best fat ferocious friends.
Now, I want you to just shut up and be delicious,"
the Woof growled, then used its warm, smelly, wet
tongue to lick a disgusting thin layer of stinky hot
saliva all over my face. (This was the worst. Its dirty
mouth germs had gotten all over me. It was unbearable.) "After I bite off your head and slurp out your
insides, I think it'll be rather fun for me to turn your
outsides into a snazzy coat for me to parade around
in. A reminder that it was I who put an end to the
lying little McFearless girl who'd never shut up."
Then the Howleewoof hoisted me above its snout
and positioned me over its salivating open mouth,
giving me a very clear, unwanted view down its
throat. There was no way I was
going to give this beast an easy
meal, so I started squirming as
wildly as I could. "Hold still so I
can bite your head off without
damaging the rest of you. Otherwise you'll ruin my coat idea,"
said one very annoyed
Howleewoof.

"NO!" I screamed as
loudly as I could.

Stink Attack

"Minerva! Minerva, where are you?" shouted Max and Ms. Monstranomicon, having heard my cry from somewhere in the distance.

"Over here! Hurry!" I screamed back at them.

Their shouts distracted the Howleewoof for only the briefest of moments. Turning his shaggy head toward the sounds, the Woof, needing an unobstructed pathway for its incredible hearing powers to work, moved me out of the way of its sensitive ears and lowered me within a fingertip's reach of Max's satchel.

"Owahrooooo!" howled the Woof, and as its howl traveled through the trees, bits of sonic information came bouncing back at him, creating pictures within the monster's head of everything within a hundred yards of him. In a matter of seconds, the Howleewoof was able to get a clear fix on Max's and Ms. Monstranomicon's exact whereabouts.

That was also all the time I needed to reach into the pack and pull out . . . a smelly pair of boots?

"They're forty yards east of here and roughly three minutes away if they hurry, but it doesn't matter. You'll be torn open by then," the Howleewoof said, chuckling and licking my entire face again with its sour-smelling slimy tongue as if I were a human lollipop, which was really the last straw.

"Hey, barf breath, I want to give you something," I said through pursed lips as I dodged his licking tongue.

"Oh, and what's that?" said the Woof.

"This!" I shouted, and punched the Howleewoof square in the nose like a boxer would have. But instead of boxing gloves, I had slipped a pair of python boots around my fists. When my punch

connected with the monster's snot-filled, greasy black nose, a fire erupted on the Woof's face and it screamed.

"Oww! Oh, no, Stinkfeet Talismans!" moaned the Howleewoof in severe pain, instantly dropping me to the ground. I was more than pleasantly surprised by the incendiary effect that the boots had on my flea-ridden foe. And I hate to admit (because of how badly I was ignored back in Whistlesqueak) how thankful I was that Max and Ms. Monstranomicon had foresightedly made up batches of the anti-Woof recipe (because if they hadn't, I probably *wouldn't* have a face).

"Who's scared of who now?" I taunted.

"Oww, it burns, you evil little brat. I'll never be able to smell again!" howled the Howleewoof, frantically patting its face with hairy hands to snuff out the flames around its snout—which caused its hands also to go up in flames. "I'll get you for this, McFearless! Mark my words, this isn't over! You are one dead child!"

"Oh, yeah? You want some more?" I threatened, and advanced toward the burning Woof. But it'd had enough and cowered away from me.

"Please, no more!" shrieked a very terrified and very flaming Howleewoof as it ran into the safety of the forest to lick its wounds.

I had done it! I had defeated my very first monster, all by myself. Where was a witness when I needed one? I had just finished that thought when I heard the slightly muffled sound of fur-covered paws clapping. I turned to see Mr. Devilstone casually resting his back against a tree.

"How long have you been standing there?" I asked, surprised.

"Long enough," he said. "Good job. You won't be seeing that monster anytime soon. Your great-great-great-grand-father would be proud of you."

"Really, you think?" I said.

"Oh, I know he would. How's your shoulder feeling, by the way? All better?" asked Mr. Devilstone, sounding concerned.

I wiggled it around before I answered him. "Perfect," I said.

"That's good; glad to hear it. Max and Ms. Monstranomicon should be here very soon, and we should set up camp for tonight. I'm sure we could all use the rest—especially you, oh, mighty monster hunter!" said Mr. Devilstone with a wink and a half-cocked, crooked smile.

When Max and Ms. Monstranomicon arrived, Max gave me my satchel,

which I was so thankful for since I'd be able to wash up. Once I had cleaned up to my satisfaction, using canteen water and a lovely lemon-scented bar of soap, I decided to tell everyone about my horrible vision. They gathered around me by the fire Mr. Devilstone had made for us, and I began. I told them of the two beasts I'd seen torturing my father— the Swoggler and the other, more supremely evil creature, which I couldn't name. Mr. Devilstone's ears perked up, and his eye began to glow a furious red. Or it could've been the reflection of the fire's crimson flames in his eyeball playing tricks on me.

"Do you know who that other monster was?" I asked curiously.

"Perhaps," said Mr. Devilstone, but I could tell he was holding something back.

"Well, do you think our father is okay?" I said, my curiosity growing.

"Perhaps," said Mr. Devilstone once again, broodingly deep in thought. Why wasn't he telling what he knew?

"Perhaps what? What do you mean?" I said, desperately confused. I knew he knew something, and I needed more of an answer than just "perhaps."

"No more questions for tonight, children," was Mr. Devilstone's response. "You both need your sleep." Then he pointed toward our tent.

Neither Max nor I was happy with the coyote's

mysterious answers, but I was too exhausted by my ordeal to argue—and Max was still very upset after hearing about my strange vision.

"Max, I want you to know that I think Dad is okay," I said with as much hope as I could muster. "And what I saw was just a dream. If he had died, I think we would've felt his passing in our hearts. And I know that I've felt no such thing. We're going to get him back."

"Yeah, I think you're right, Mini," Max said as he wiped away a tear. Then he grabbed me and hugged me as hard as he could. His loving gesture strengthened the belief I had in my own words, and I squeezed him back even harder.

So Max and I grabbed some blankets and snuggled up with Ms. Monstranomicon. I was pretty sure that the Howleewoof wouldn't show his mangy face around there again, but I decided to read up on the beast, just in case.

⟡ THE HOWLEEWOOF ⟡

A coarse-haired, inhumanoidal wolflike creature with keen monster-enhanced animal senses. Normally born five to a litter, they are of varying color, depending on their geographical environment. When full-grown, they stand between seven and eight feet tall. Possessing huge yellow eyes that allow them to see in the dark and a powerful muzzle filled with two sets of fangs designed for ripping and tearing human flesh, these monsters are some of the fiercest and most agile creatures of our kind. Physically they are strong, but they are prone to low self-esteem. They are serious stalkers, with razor-sharp, elongated fingernails, useful for all sorts of slashings and slayings. They have an incredible ability to track prey from hundreds of miles away due to their supremely superior sense of smell, and they can climb up any surface to reach their victims. The Howleewoof, or Woof for short, seldom bathes, resulting in flea infestations and mange. Most have a unique flair for cooking and an unnatural fascination with fashion. Some enjoy collecting articles of clothing worn by their devoured victims, and in rare cases, more artistic Woofs enjoy transforming the remains of their meals into monster clothing, which they proudly wear around monster-infested townships. Their only natural enemies, besides sunlight, are larger, more deadly monsters, angry swarms of humans and the awful snout-burning properties of Stinkfeet Talismans.

A defensive recipe:

THE STINKFEET TALISMANS

You will need:

- 1 cauldron (or large mixing bowl)
- 1 tabletop
- 1 pair of human hands
- 1 nose to sniff with
- 2 of your own bare stinky feet (the stinkier they are, the more powerful the talismans will be)
- 1 opened can of tuna fish
- 1 cup of toilet water
- 6 pieces of stinky, moldy cheese (the stinkier and moldier it is, the more powerful the talismans will be)
- 4 scoops of mustard (any kind will do, but the stinkier it is, the more powerful the talismans will be)
- 12 pinches of baker's yeast (any kind will do, but the stinkier it is, the more powerful the talismans will be)
- 1 pair of python boots (for maximum strength) or, if unavailable, 1 pair of any other ordinary shoes (not as powerful but still effective)
- 1 timepiece for measuring time

Place the cauldron or large mixing bowl onto the tabletop. Carefully combine the tuna fish, toilet water, stinky, moldy cheese, mustard and baker's yeast in your cauldron. With human hands, lightly mix the contents together. Sniff with your nose the fresh new stench being created, which is now stuck all over your fingers, and try not to barf. Next, divide the stinky contents of the cauldron up into 2 equal parts to place into the python boots (or any other, ordinary pair of shoes). Using your left human hand only, place one part of the mixture into the right python boot, and with your right human hand only, place the other half of the mixture into the left python boot. Finally, place your own 2 bare feet into the opposite-corresponding python boots (left foot into the right boot, and left boot onto the right foot). Begin squishing the stinky, tuna-fishy mixture between your toes and shout at the top of your lungs *"Peeyoo stinkfeet zoowoo cha, peeyoozoowoo stinkfeet zacha wahza ha cha cha"* while walking around in the boots for 6 minutes. After the proper amount of time has passed according to your timepiece, the Stinkfeet Talismans will be finished and will have become quite deadly to a Howleewoof. The smell of one alone can keep a family safe from being

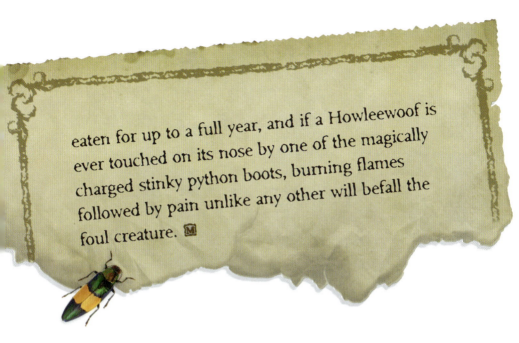

eaten for up to a full year, and if a Howleewoof is ever touched on its nose by one of the magically charged stinky python boots, burning flames followed by pain unlike any other will befall the foul creature. M

As I lay there, imagining the constellations above us, I really began to miss my mother—and feared for my dad's safety even more. But having Max by my side helped a lot and brought comfort to my worrying mind. It took me a while, but I finally fell asleep, holding Max's hand.

My Moldy Midafternoon

*T*he moment the sun rose, Ms. Monstranomicon was already back in her protective sack, and Max and I went to work on packing up the campsite for the long walk ahead of us. The morning and afternoon were pretty uneventful, except for the weather. It changed dramatically, going from muggy to muggier, then settling into the muggiest, most uncomfortable climate one could ever go hiking around in.

As we made our way toward the Marshlands of Mold's polluted muddy waters, Max wouldn't stop talking about *pirates*! Since he'd never been on a boat before, Max kept wondering out loud about what we might use to cross the murky

depths. In his mind, there'd be a giant pirate ship with his name on it, waiting patiently for its captain (Max). I hate it when he's in pirate mode, and he was in it full force that day. "All ye chickenhearted land-lubbers can't catch me, for I am the dreaded pirate Maxwell McFearless, captain of the stormy seven seas." I felt like stuffing my sweaty feet-flavored socks down Max's pirate throat, I wanted him to shut up so bad. But I didn't have to.

Thankfully, he shut himself up once we made it to our shallow swampland destination. He was so disappointed by how unlike an ocean it was, he was rendered speechless. I guess the dreaded pirate Maxwell McFearless, sadly, would have to set sail some other time. But I too was upset, for different reasons. The mosquito-riddled watery wasteland before me was worse than I ever could have possibly imagined. Noxious fumes invaded our noses, and biting bugs nibbled at our warm necks. I hated the thick spoiled-egg smell of it all. Only insects and alligators could survive these queasy conditions year-round. Humans weren't made, in my McFearless estimation, to withstand much time in these polluted parts.

I couldn't take it anymore. I searched through our satchels and found some extra pieces of clothing. I quickly tore a cotton undershirt into two pieces and tied half around my nose and mouth, trying to cover as much of my face as possible. Then I held the other half of the shirt out to Max and instructed him to do the same. But he just stared at me like I was a crazy person. I figured the fabric would act as a filter and keep most of the miserable marshland's harmful inhalants out of our systems. Then I rolled down my sleeves to my wrists, even though the temperature was extremely warm, pulled my socks up as high as they would go and piled on layers of clothing until the only parts of me not covered were my hands and a slit around my eyes so that I could see. I wished that this weren't the case, that I'd had the foresight to bring gloves and goggles. I was sure that I looked like some sort of strange Bedouin child or an escapee from an insane asylum, but I didn't care. I didn't want the diseases that the Marshlands of Mold could give me.

Max just stood there and laughed.

"I must admit that Max is right; you do look silly, Minerva," Mr. Devilstone said with a giggle. "It does smell rather putrid around here, but there is no need for you to cover up in the way that you have. There's a higher chance of being eaten by a monster than catching a disease. So take all that silly stuff off." I had a hard time caring about Mr. Devilstone's opinions at that moment because he was the one who had suggested that we take this disgusting route, and so far there had been no sign of my father, just monsters. I had to wonder if we were just being taken on some wild-goose chase, conducted by a mean, mysterious coyote, for no reason. I was angry, worried, confused, hungry and fed up. Plus, it was hard to breathe with all that cloth I had around my face.

"Okay, enough is enough, Mr. Devilstone. I want answers, and I want them now!" I demanded.

"What can I help you with, Minerva? Knowing you, I'm sure there's a list," he said, and rolled his eye.

"Well, for starters, how are we going to get across this disgusting place?" I asked, a little impolitely.

"I'm meeting a friend here who's going to help us all cross. I'm sure he'll be along any moment now," answered Mr. Devilstone. "Is there anything else you would like to ask me in a more courteous manner?"

"Yes, as a matter of fact. Why won't you answer my questions about my father and that mysterious monster from my vision? I'm worried about my

father, I'm worried about our safety and I think you're hiding something. Maybe I was right about you from the beginning. Maybe you are working for . . . *monsters!* Behind you, look out!" I screamed, and grabbed Max.

From the depths of the stagnant, watery sludge emerged not just one but *three* Moldrens!

The mossy, mold-encrusted creatures crept out from the marsh toward us, all of them in varying shades of green and brown, each one bigger than the one before. They each had three eyes and bacteria-filled mouths crammed full of teeth at least triple the size of a human's. Their wet, over-grown, rabbitlike noses constantly twitched and dripped disease. Their disgusting mold-covered

arms were the size of fallen tree trunks, and their legs seemed twice as massive. Puddles formed with every step they took toward us as the murky waters squirted through the toes of their hooflike, rhinocerous-sized feet. The idea of any of them touching me with their moldy hands made me want to scream, and one of the Moldrens wouldn't stop staring at me with all three of its creepy eyes.

Then Mr. Devilstone did something I hadn't expected. He almost keeled over, he laughed so hard. Max grabbed Ms. Monstranomicon and we ran as fast as we could. We needed to find a way out of the marshlands alive. Our hearts beating fast and our legs pumping hard, Max and I ran neck and neck against the acrid air—until his foot snagged a vine and he tumbled to the ground. It took me a second to realize that he was down, and when I stopped to go back for him, I noticed that Mr. Devilstone was casually standing right behind me. In the distance, I saw Max and Ms. Monstranomicon slumped over the shoulder of one of the Moldrens, being carried back toward the polluted water's edge.

"Minerva, I am not your enemy and you are never going to find your father if you go in that direction. That I'm sure of," said Mr. Devilstone calmly.

"How can I trust you?" I asked, all panicky.

"Your brother is in no danger and neither are

you, Minerva. Now listen to me," he said gently, and placed a paw on my shoulder. "I know you have questions and I promise I'll answer all of them, once we get your father back." Then he seized my hand. "You have my word, Minerva: no harm will befall a McFearless as long as I shall live." With a blink of his only eye and a burst of red lightning, suddenly the world around me ceased to exist. Time and space seemed to fold in on themselves. I felt like I was moving faster than I'd ever moved before, without actually moving at all. I'd been magically transported back to the water's edge and was surrounded by Moldrens. Max greeted me with a smile, unlike any I'd ever seen before, plastered on his face.

Max's Moldren-Made Smile

Max's smile made more sense once I stopped staring at the Moldrens and looked at the shoreline. For a second I had thought his smile might be for me, but it wasn't. It was directed toward something he'd always wanted, something he'd always talked about—a pirate ship! I couldn't care less about his pirate fantasies, but this was amazing. The ship was rapidly being built—no, not *built,* that's not the right word. It was *growing* out of the water. All sorts of plants, molds and spores fused together into the shape of a pirate ship right before our eyes.

Max was in heaven, and it seemed that I had been wrong about a couple of things that I'd like to clarify:

1) Pirate ships in marshlands—apparently there are some.
2) Not all Moldrens are evil. That's according to Ms. Monstranomicon's page 430.

✦ THE MOLDREN ✦

These one-of-a-kind mold-covered creatures stand out from other monster breeds due to their unique powers, unlimited sun-withstanding capabilities and vegetarianism (the exception being bacon). They often live in waterlogged areas of land, beside polluted water with poor drainage. They despise well-manicured lawns as well as beautifully maintained gardens and enjoy nothing more than their destruction. Moldrens have incredible regenerative powers. As long as their heads remain intact after an attack, they can regenerate all of their body parts. They also possess fantastic telepathic powers that enable them to control and command all manner of plant life to do their bidding, granting them the ability to create objects of any shape, size or complexity, then give them lives of their own (e.g., transforming something as simple as a bush into something as useful as a rocking chair that enjoys rubbing feet). Unlike other monsters, who find sunlight harmful and deadly, Moldrens need the sun to survive. During the daylight hours, they absorb the sun's nutrients. These nutrients account for half of their dietary needs. The rest of their diet consists of the toxic pollutants found in their nearby water sources and occasional slices of fried pig flesh. They are exceptional swimmers and not well liked by most of the monster community because of their neutral position on human affairs. Moldrens are, for the most part, antisocial monsters, preferring the solitude of their marshlands to the company of others. But in rare situations, some have had friendships with humans. They are vulnerable only to fire and the Soap Scum Spray Serum.

A defensive recipe:

Soap Scum Spray Serum

You will need:

- 1 mouth for chewing and spitting
- 1 cauldron (or large mixing bowl)
- 1 wooden spoon
- 1 empty spray bottle
- 13 chocolate chips
- 4 freshly picked boogers (the more you pick, the more powerful the Soap Scum Spray Serum will be)
- Juice from 3 moldy brown lemons
- 1 cup of used and undrained soapy bathwater
- 1 timepiece for measuring time

Put all 13 chocolate chips in your mouth and finely chew without swallowing any of the chocolaty goodness. Keep chewing until a fine chocolaty saliva paste is formed, then spit it into your cauldron or large mixing bowl while making loud barfing noises. Next, place (at least) 4 fresh-picked boogers into the cauldron. Then add the juice from the moldy brown lemons and the used and undrained soapy bathwater to the cauldron. With your wooden spoon, stir the contents of your cauldron together for 2 minutes and not a second longer. You will know that it is done when the water turns an ugly shade of brown with boogers floating around in it. Next, pour the contents of your cauldron into the empty spray bottle and say these magic words: *Smellah zeetle poof, ambrah gastra goop, raccoon hands and frying pans, moldy Moldrens too.* Your Soap Scum Spray Serum is now ready. Go outside and squirt the Soap Scum Spray Serum (a little goes a long way) around the entire property line of your home, every 5 feet, to protect it for one whole year against Moldrens. Ⓜ

I calmed down once I learned that Moldrens didn't like to eat people, but got incredibly angry when I found out that the biggest Moldren had taken part in my father's kidnapping. So I kicked it as hard as I could in the leg. A large chunk broke

off and stuck to my shoe, spurting a watery, green, bloodlike liquid all over the place.

"Ow!" shouted the Moldren, and saplike tears slowly started dripping from all three of its eyes. The other two Moldrens snarled defensively and were about to retaliate, but the big Moldren called them off.

"That was for my father, and if you know what's good for you, you'll give him back!" I yelled through my face cloth. I geared up to sock it in its crying third eye, but Mr. Devilstone stopped me.

"Don't you dare strike Milgrew again," the coyote scolded. "If it weren't for him, your father would probably be dead by now. Apologize at once, Minerva."

"No, little one, you have every reason to be angry," sighed Milgrew the Moldren. Then he commanded the parts of himself still stuck to my shoe to crawl back onto his leg where they belonged. In no time whatsoever, the place where I'd injured him had healed itself. "I probably deserved that kick. But you must understand something, Minerva. I've been working undercover as a monster double agent for years now, supplying humans, like your family, for instance, with important monster information. Please believe me when I say that I only participated in your father's kidnapping so that I could hopefully ensure his safety. I wanted to set your father free and pretend that he'd somehow escaped, but that

insidious Snargle who accompanied me to your father's incarceration watched him far too closely for that. Unfortunately, my monsters on the inside have relayed to me that your father has been swoggled and that Medighouls had to be brought in to repair his badly battered broken body. There's no word yet on exactly what sort of mental state the swoggling has left him in but, at least for now, he is alive. That is why I feel it is I who should apologize to you and your brother, for not being able to do more for him. Hopefully, together, we can make things right. I've enlisted the help of my Moldren comrades-in-arms, Sporak and Mushroach, in the building of a mighty McFearless vessel that will carry us all safely to the burning sands of Skullbury Desert. I hope that this makes up for at least some of the grief I have caused your family and that someday you might find it in your hearts to forgive me."

✥ The Medighoul ✥

These are the earthbound spirits of long-dead doctors, witch doctors, veterinarians, shamans, dentists, healers, voodoo priests and other medical professionals who lost their lives after being savagely attacked by a bloodthirsty monster. Confused, bodiless and horrible to look at, Medighouls are doomed forever to float the earth, doing the only thing their ghost minds can remember—practicing medicine. These ghoulish doctors possess the bodies of the sick or injured for a limited amount of time, which rapidly heals their patients' ailments but leaves them covered from head to toe in goopy ectoplasm. Since they are undead, Medighouls do not need to eat to survive. Occasionally, however, they do get the munchies and like to bite the toes off little children.

A defensive recipe:

Miracle Sneeze

You will need:

- 🦇 1 cauldron (or large mixing bowl)
- 🦇 1 human nose for sneezing
- 🦇 1 wooden spoon

- 8 tablespoons of ground pepper
- 1 apple
- 25 sneezes

Place the ground pepper in your cauldron or large mixing bowl. Mix rapidly with the wooden spoon and count backward from 15. Next, put your nose as close as you can to the ground pepper and take several deep breaths. This should make you want to sneeze. Quickly grab the apple and sneeze all over it 25 times. After you've finished sneezing, say this magic word: *Temhasineam!* Place the Miracle Sneezed-upon apple in the center of your home and leave it there until it rots. You will be Medighoul-safe for 9 months. 🄼

Milgrew's words made me feel tremendous shame for the way I had acted. I never should have kicked him. "I am so sorry for what I did to you," I told him sincerely. "And I thank you very much for all that you've done."

"It only hurt for a moment. See? I've put myself back together again. So don't worry," replied Milgrew sweetly.

"Can we please just get on the boat and save our dad already?" implored Max. It was obvious to everyone that Max couldn't wait any longer to climb aboard his fantasy fulfilled.

"Well, it seems that Max here is extremely fond of the boat we've made, which gives me an idea," said Milgrew. He searched inside his ears with his long, twiglike fingernails and plucked out a thin, needlelike thorn. "Do you trust me, little pirate captain?" asked Milgrew.

"Um, yeah, I do, sort of," replied Max, without need of a gum ball.

"Good. I'll try to make this as painless as I can," said Milgrew. "Stick out a finger." Max did as he was told and closed his eyes. Then Milgrew pricked his finger with the thorn.

"Did you do it yet?" asked Max, eyes still closed. He hadn't felt a thing, yet his finger had the tiniest droplet of blood on it.

"Yes, it is done, young sea captain. You can open your eyes now," answered Milgrew.

"Why'd you do that?" I asked. "I mean, what was the point?"

"Well, Minerva, I did it so that I could give your brother a present I think he'll really enjoy. I have infected him with parts of me."

Hearing that made Max need a gum ball right away.

Milgrew realized he'd caused my brother fear, which was not his intent. So he explained to Max reassuringly what a truly magical thing he had done for him. A thing that, to Milgrew's knowledge, had never been done for a human before. "Max, don't be nervous. Think of this thorn of mine with your blood on it as a key. Now, once I place this 'key' into the ship's steering wheel, it will only ever serve one human master, and that person shall be you, young Maxwell McFearless. It'll never set sail without you, and it'll always be loyal only to you. Wherever you want to go, it'll take you, and when you need it, it will come. I suspect it'll do whatever you

want it to, Max, because I believe that you have it in you to be the greatest sea captain of them all."

Max loved hearing that. His mind had been blown away, as if it had been blasted with a pirate's cannonball. The ship was everything he had ever hoped for, with two massive oak trees for masts, one fore and one aft. Their smooth branches held leaves that were woven tightly into green sails set lengthwise along the golden-brown wooden deck. The ship could easily carry up to fifty-five crewmen or twenty-five crewmonsters comfortably and would still have more than enough room for plenty of piles of pirate booty. With eight mounted self-loading monster-designed cannons and four fearsome swivel guns at its devilish disposal, it was a living, sailing terror, and it looked like it could move faster than the wind itself.

(Max got his dream boat; I got scary, uncontrollable visions. Great!)

"Milgrew . . ." Tears of joy welled up in Max's eyes. "This is the greatest thing ever. Thank you, thank you, thank you."

"Wait," Milgrew said. "It will need one other thing. A name. So how about it, Max?"

Max quieted down, paused for a moment and chose a name for his boat. "I think she should be called *Adelaide,* after my mother. It was her middle name," he explained to Milgrew. Then he actually

hugged the moldy monster. Gross.

"*Adelaide* it is, then," declared Milgrew with kindness in his face. He patted Max softly on his head; then he closed all three of his eyes and sent out a telepathic message. Max shook his head slightly, as if he had a bumble-bee stuck inside it. He could hear what Milgrew was thinking at him, and it caught him a little off guard. "Max, this is how you'll be able to communicate with your ship," said Milgrew with his brain. "You try it now. Ask me something."

Max scrunched up his forehead hard in concentration and squeezed his brain waves right through the top of his head. "Can you hear me? Am I doing this right?"

"Yes. Loud and clear, young sea captain," responded Milgrew, impressed. "Now, cast your eyes back toward your boat, for she knows her name and wears it proudly."

Max turned just in time to see the last letters of the name he had given the ship magically appear, in bright sea-foam-green lettering, boldly across her starboard bow.

Like I said before, it was truly amazing (not that I'm jealous).

Sailing Toward a Snargle

cMax was a fine captain indeed. He had read so many books on the subjects of sailing and piracy that he was a natural at the helm—except that the rocking of the boat made him violently ill. "I'll get used to it," he kept saying between bouts of barfing over the side. "This probably happened to every great sea captain the first time he sailed, Minerva. Don't laugh at me. It's not funny," he begged between barfs. But I couldn't stop. I felt that there was finally justice in the world, and I wanted to relish Max's suffering for as long as I could before he adjusted to the wobbling of the waves.

Ms. Monstranomicon was sitting with Mr. Devilstone belowdecks in the crew's quarters, discussing what to do once we reached the desert. We all talked for a bit and I read from Ms. Monstranomicon out loud, the way she liked. It was all very pleasant for once. I had thought that our

travel time would be longer for some reason, but Mr. Devilstone informed me that we'd probably reach our scorching, sand-filled destination just before daybreak and suggested I get some rest. I took his advice and bid everyone good night. I found a nice place to rest my head in the captain's chamber, where I closed my eyes and fell fast asleep.

Mr. Devilstone woke me a few hours later by scratching and biting my feet. He seemed a bit stranger than usual.

"Minerva, I hope you had a splendid nap. Sorry to have woken you," he said. "I want you to hide Ms. Monstranomicon under your clothes. You have enough of them on, so it shouldn't be a problem. I lost her sack somehow and I wouldn't want her to get burnt by the sun's rays in the desert. Do you mind?"

"No, I guess not," I told him as the boat suddenly shook hard.

"I think you should do it now," he said, and handed her to me. "One more thing: beware of the Zarmaglorg! Things aren't always what they seem. Be brave and keep your wits about you."

The Enotslived Diamond was glowing more brightly than I'd ever seen it glow before, yet what it meant never registered in my mind—until it was too late. A Snargleflougasaurus battered down the door to our room, grabbed Mr. Devilstone and gob-

bled him down, crunch after bone-cracking crunch. It happened so fast, Mr. Devilstone didn't have a chance.

"Nooooooo!" I screamed.

"Mmh, me favorite meat be coyote for Snargle," mumbled the Snargleflougasaurus—and that was when I noticed that it had my brother in its clawed hand. Max was unconscious and his head looked like it had been bashed.

"Oh, no! Max! Max, can you hear me?" I yelled. "Max, wake up! Oh, no! You've killed him!"

"Me no kill him boy brother. Me only do what master say me do. I do to you now, girl sister, like what me already done to boy brother him," said the Snargleflougasaurus, and it hit me awfully hard in the face with its bulbous spiked tail. I was knocked out cold.

Back to the Beginning of the End

Congratulations are in order! You are now officially caught up as to how Max and I managed to find ourselves dangling in a giant ironclad birdcage suspended over a bottomless pit of fire. I wish I could offer whoever is reading this a prize for sifting through my McFearlessly monstrous memoirs, but I'm a little preoccupied with finishing my story at the moment.

Like I mentioned in my first chapter, an explosion of tremendous fury had burst forth from the odious depths of the flaming chasm below us and sent our cages crashing into each other. And after all the smoke had cleared, I determined these three things:

1) We were still breathing. (Good.)
2) The lock on our cage was busted. (Really good.)

3) The Snargle was finished with its nap. (Not so good.)

Once our cages stopped swinging wildly, I looked down at Max, who was rubbing his jaw, and I saw one of the saddest things ever. A flaming dead baby bat that had caught its end from the fiery blast had landed, toasted and cooked, by Max's foot. I thought it was still adorable, in a burnt-up kind of way, with its wings smoldering. Max didn't think so. He looked at it and grimaced, then kicked its cute carcass over the side of the cage and into the pit below. Jerk.

I guessed Max didn't feel so great after being ping-ponged around our birdcage cell by the explosion. I had on layer after layer of shock-absorbing fabric to protect me, but Max had nothing to soften

the barrage of blows he had sustained. Oh, and I almost forgot, Ms. Monstranomicon was shoved up the back of my shirt too, which really helped, because she took the brunt of the beatings for me. I was sure she felt like thousands of pages of pulverized swollen gibberish right about then, since she was the one who had broken the lock of our cage with her spine.

"Children, are you all right? Minerva? Max?" asked Ms. Monstranomicon between small panicked grunts of pain and frantic page ruffles that tickled my back. "Oh, please get me out of here. I don't want to be eaten by a Snargle. Can you hear me?"

I gently pulled her out from under my shirt and held her low, toward the bottom of our cell, so that the Snargle wouldn't see her. "Ms. Monstranomicon, I'm okay, but how are you doing?"

"I'll live, but I suspect not for long if the Zarmaglorg knows that I'm here," said Ms. Monstranomicon. "You were both unconscious for so long and that Snargleflougasaurus was so mean to you, I was terrified. I wanted to try to escape and go for help, but I was way too scared that the Snargle would eat me like it ate Mr. Devilstone. How are we ever going to get out of here?"

"Who are you talking to in there, Minerva?" asked my father from across the way. He was straining his neck to get a better view of who it was and what we were doing. "I'm worried about you, my precious, adorable baby girl. If anything had happened to either of you, I don't think I would have been able to go on. Now, Daddy wants to know who is in there with you, okay, my little lamb chops?" Our father sounded like he'd been hit on the head one too many times. It wasn't like him to talk that way. I mean, it was weird. I tried to answer him, but the Snargleflougasaurus was curious too.

"I see sister boy mouths moving, girl and boy brother sister, why be talking? Me no can hear you. If Snargle no can hear then me want quiet so not one body hear. Girl boy sister brother shut mouth now!" shouted the Snargle furiously. Ms. Monstranomicon was so terrified of being discovered, she gasped once and fainted.

"Okay!" Max and I yelled down to the Snargle.

"Me no hear you, what boy girl say?" roared the hard-of-hearing Snargle back up at us.

"We said we'll be quiet!" Max and I hollered as loudly as we could.

"Good boy girl sister brother. I go get master now so he reward me Snargle food. Me tummy no like coyote me had. Me have pain down in tummy place, Snargle no like bad feeling. Boy girl meat maybe fix Snargle tummy problem, me go ask master for permission to eat sister boy meat now," said the Snargle as it lumbered off.

✦ The Snargleflougasaurus ✦

These monsters of low-level intelligence often suffer serious bellyaches and are prone to hellacious forms of halitosis. Their diet includes baby-duck bills, camel humps and human children, but their absolute favorite meal is coyote. They are one of the strongest breeds of monster on the planet and have hides tough enough to withstand speeding spears, arsenals of arrows, rockslides and lightning. Most are hard of hearing and prefer silence at all times. Snargles have extremely limited vocabularies, so they communicate through the use of excessive violence. They are quickly agitated creatures and often throw unnecessary temper tantrums. They prefer servitude as a way of life and are fiercely loyal to their masters. Their favorite pastimes include sniffing the rear ends of other Snargleflougasauri, belching while passing gas and licking hairy armpits. Often yellow or blue, Snargles are easily recognizable by their garish spots and their massive macelike tails.

Their only enemies are

sunlight, their own stupidity and the Mudworm Moonbiscuit.

A defensive recipe:
MUDWORM MOONBISCUIT

You will need:

- 1 cauldron (or large mixing bowl)
- 1 pair of human hands
- 3 cups of all-purpose flour
- 1 cup of dirt
- 5 tablespoons of salt
- 11 teaspoons of orange juice
- 1 cup of milk
- 1 long tube sock
- 7 hours (at least) of direct moonlight
- 1 timepiece for measuring time

In the cauldron or large mixing bowl, place the all-purpose flour, dirt and salt. Mix the contents with human hands until it is all one color. Then, while holding your breath, add the orange juice and milk. (If you fail to hold your breath while adding these ingredients, you must start all over from the beginning.) Once again, mix the contents with human hands until the mixture is extra-squishy and sticks to your fingers like mud. Place the contents of your cauldron inside the long tube sock, smush them all to the bottom and tie the top of the sock into a knot.

Then take the wormlike stuffed sock outside and leave it in direct moonlight for at least 7 hours to absorb its rays. Say these magic words: *Snargle, poozum, wiplowbius, merp, Snargle gohbibi seeyoogoh perpfy.* Then place the Mudworm Moonbiscuit under your sofa like a hidden worm to protect your entire household from Snargles for one whole year. Ⓜ

The Snargle headed toward a large jagged opening in the cavern wall. Inside I could see a few steps of a small staircase that I assumed led up into the haunted stone walls of Castle Doominstinkinfart. It was unusual to see the enormous Snargle trying to make its way up the tiny stairs with its monstrously sized body. It was slow going, and the Snargle had to bend its peanut-sized-brain-filled head down close to its elephant-looking scaled feet going up the narrow passageway. There was no other exit in the cavern, unless you considered falling to our deaths a way out. We needed to escape and I had a plan.

"Children, the Snargle is gone now. Don't be afraid. Tell me who you were talking to, please," said my father. I thought he'd be angry and disappointed that I had inadvertently smuggled Ms. Monstranomicon back into that evil place, so I lied.

"Nobody, Dad. It's just Max and me in here," I said, hoping I was convincing. Then I handed Ms. Monstranomicon to Max and shot him a look like "If you tell on me right now, I'll kill you."

"But I heard someone else in there with you. Are you sure you're not lying to me, pumpkin?" There was something in the way my father said *pumpkin* that gave me the creeps.

"Yeah, I'm sure, Daddy," I said, and Max even kept his mouth closed for once. "I have an idea about how to get out of here. Just give Max and me a few minutes, okay?" I said, changing the subject.

"No, children, stay where you are! It is too dangerous for you," my father ordered.

But I was already taking action. I had no intention of staying in our filthy birdcage prison a moment longer. "Sorry, Daddy, but I have to try something. Just hold on," I said.

"Max, Minerva, no! Do you hear me? No!" my father commanded, but I just tuned him out. Max was definitely torn between obeying our father and getting out of our cage.

The desire to escape won him over.

Our cages were suspended by ancient, rusty

chains attached to a worn-down swing arm. I guessed the arm could be used to move the cages right, left, up or down. The controls to the swing-arm mechanism, consisting of several levers and a turn wheel, were a good fifty feet away. So my plan was to make a line of rope from the extra clothes I had on (once again proving useful) long enough for Max to be able to lower me down from our cage. Then I would try to swing myself safely over to solid ground—without the rope breaking and me falling to a hideously painful burning death, of course. When I told Max what I intended to do, he offered me a gum ball. Then we got to work.

Max helped me rip the clothing up into long strips. Then we knotted them together into one long, multicolored, multi-textured rope. We secured one end of it to one of the lowest bars of our cage, close to the cage door. The door was barely held closed by its busted lock, and all that was needed to open it was a hard push. But Max decided he had to finish the job by unnecessarily kicking it open, scarily resulting in his almost tumbling out. (That would not have been fun.) I had to grab Max by his belt loops to save him.

"Thanks, Minerva, that was almost the end of me," said Max, shaking and sweating.

"Maxwell and Minerva, I want you both

to stop what you're doing this very instant, do you hear me? You are both too young to be daredeviling around like that with your lives, my little cupcakes!" screamed our father, but it made no difference.

"Max, I need you right now," I said firmly, snapping him out of his daze.

"I'm here, I'm ready. Are you sure you want to do this, Minerva?" asked Max, cautiously looking over the side where he had just almost fallen, where I was willingly intending to go.

"No, Max, I don't really want to. It's scary. But someone has to, so help me over the side before I lose my nerve." I wrapped my end of the rope around my wrists and held on tightly.

Max picked up the remaining slack of the rope in both his hands and anchored his feet to the sides of the open cage door. "Don't worry, Mini, I've got you."

I took several deep breaths to calm my rapidly beating heart. "On the count of three. One, two, three!" Then I stepped off into nothing.

Max jerked slightly from my weight as he held on, lowering me inch by inch toward the flaming abyss below. I couldn't look beneath me for fear that a petrifying panic would take over my body. I imagined myself as a hooked piece of bait, powerlessly

snared on the end of a fishing wire, intended to lure death's burning jaws around me for a nine-year-old struggling fisherman. I had to stay focused on my plan. I needed to save my brother and father. I wanted to go home. So once I heard Max shout down from above me, "That's as far as you can go, Minerva," I began to swing. The knots were holding, but my hands were getting tired. I had only one shot at this, so I needed to make it count. I focused on my target of solid, sturdy ground. I swung my legs high above my head, forcing my weight as far forward as possible. I became a human pendulum swinging back and forth, gaining speed, height and momentum as I went. I had to cover a great distance with a length of rope fifteen feet short of my intended target, so the rest would have to be made up in the air. I waited until I was going as high and fast as I could, until I felt like I couldn't hold on to the rope any longer—and that was when I let go, launching myself through the air, the heat of the demon flames beckoning below. It wasn't a graceful landing, and I certainly wouldn't want to try something like that ever again, but I made it—alive and uncooked.

"Great job, Minerva. Now get us down from here," shouted Max, relieved by my success. But strangely, our father said nothing.

"Two safely lowered cages coming right up!" I

shouted at them, dusting myself off from my not-so-soft landing. An inventory of my scrapes would have to wait. With all my strength, I pulled the proper levers and turned the wheel to lower the cages safely. Before Max's cage touched down, he jumped the last few inches with Ms. Monstranomicon in his hands and ran toward me.

"Yes! You were awesome, Minerva. Great job!" He tackled me with a hug and squeezed me like only a little brother could.

"How did we get down here?" asked Ms. Monstranomicon groggily, finally waking up.

"I can't believe you woke up just now and you missed all the scary bits I had to go through. I'll tell you all about it in a second. Let me free my dad," I told the book as I worked the levers. My father's cage must not have had a lock on it, because once it touched ground, he flung his cell door wide open and came straight toward me.

"Now, Daddy, don't be mad, but Ms. Monstranomicon is here with us. I know you said that if she were ever to fall back into the hands of evil, there was no telling what monsters would be able to do. That's why we need to get out of here as fast as possible, before the Snargle comes back. So don't be mad, okay?"

"Minerva, Max, I am not mad

about Ms. Monstranomicon being here. Quite the opposite, and I'm so glad that both of you are safe. I would have hated it if either of you had fallen into that dreadful pit, my sweet lumps," he said, wrapping his arms around Max and me, squeezing us tightly. We closed our eyes and hugged him back. His arms grew tighter and tighter as he held us close to him. "I would have cried my eyes out if I had lost the chance to SSssuck SSssyour SSssbrainsSS, SSssand SSssmy SSssmaster SSsswill SSssbe SSsspleased SSssto SSsshave SSssthe SSsstraitorousSS SSssbook SSssback."

All at once the awful truth reared its ugly head—and I do mean ugly. What we'd thought to be

our father morphed back into its true form, the Swoggler—the same creature that had drained my poor father to within an inch of his life.

Max and I had been hornswoggled by a Swoggler.

What had once been our father's arms were now leeching tentacles with bitey mouths. What had once been our father's worried face was now a gaping sucker maw filled with serrated needle teeth, smothered in slime, with saber-tooth tusks protruding from its undulating lips. Max and I kicked and screamed while it salivated in sheer delight at our horror. Ms. Monstranomicon promptly fainted once again, useless, and was snatched up by one of the Swoggler's free tentacles. I couldn't help thinking that after all we had been through, after all that we had risked, Max and I would sadly soon be dead—eaten slowly by a Swoggler.

The King of Evil

"*I* told you not to eat them, you insubordinate fool! Not until I have questioned them myself. Take them out of your mouths at once and put them down," commanded a towering beast, interrupting the Swoggler's feast. "And hand me that traitorous book!" The startled Swoggler lowered us to the ground and handed Ms. Monstranomicon to its master.

"SSssyesSS, SSssmaster. SSssorry, SSssmaster. SSssforgive SSssme, SSssmaster," slurped the Swoggler obediently.

We were momentarily spared the cruelty of being eaten, only to face a more horrible monster and possibly a more horrible fate. The Snargle had returned with the terrifying creature from my vision—the nightmarish shark-eyed gargoyle.

"Wake up, you traitorous tome. Your old master commands you!" spoke the creature with a voice like hot oil dripping on our eardrums. A

dark, crackling energy shot from its eyes, enveloping Ms. Monstranomicon in harmful hatred.

"I'm burning, I'm burning!" screamed a struggling, smoldering Ms. Monstranomicon. "Oh, no! Not you again, never you! You are so cruel; my worst nightmare has come true again. Run, children, run!" But there was nowhere for us to go. We were trapped between three abominable creatures who had no plans to let us escape.

"Stop hurting her, you fiend!" I yelled.

"How touching, the girl really seems to care about you, traitor," said the beast.

"Please let them go," pleaded Ms. Monstranomicon. "I'll stay with you forever, I'll give freely all the secrets I possess. Just let them live. They're only children."

"Shut up, book! You don't get to tell the king of evil what he should or should not do!" growled the villainous creature as it ripped half of her pages out and flung her to the ground, where she lay motionless, silently bleeding all her ink.

"No!" I cried. Max and I stood slack-jawed as we stared at our deeply wounded friend, not sure if she was alive or dead.

"I'm so sorry to have kept you two McFearless mischief-makers waiting, but now that I've taken care of reacquainting myself with an old friend, you have my undivided attention," the beast said.

"Allow me to properly introduce my royally evil self. I am the Zarmaglorg, the king of evil, and I must say, what a pleasure it is to finally meet both of you."

"Go stand in the sun!" I shouted.

"That was very funny, McFearless. Almost as funny as when I tortured your father and beat him senseless. Now, you have something that I desperately want, so why don't we get down to business?"

"Snargle want coyote-in-belly pain go bye-bye," moaned the Snargle. "Me want girl boy sister meat. Me thinks brother sister meaty boy girl bones help Snargle pain disappear. Please, master, let Snargle eat!"

"SSssyesSS, SSssmaster, SSsslet SSssme SSsstaste SSsstheir SSssdeliciousss SSssthoughtsSS. SSsslet SSssme SSsswoggle SSssthe SSsslife SSssout SSssof SSssthem, SSssmaster," hissed the Swoggler hungrily.

"Well, it seems that both my Snargle and my Swoggler are very eager to eat the two of you, which leaves me in a bind, because I also need answers out of you. What should I do, I wonder? I want to be a good king to my starving, suffering servants, but I also want to be your friend, children, to give you the opportunity to escape their savage swoggling and snargling. Would you like that? All you have to do is tell me where the Enotslived Diamond is and I'll let you go," the Zarmaglorg bargained.

"Yes, that would be really great. I would like very much to live," said Max, stuffing two gum balls into his mouth.

"That is a very sensible decision, young Maxwell. That is your name, correct?" asked the Zarmaglorg.

"Yes, it is, Mr. King of Evil, Zarmaglorg, sir. But I have no idea what an Enotslived Diamond is," answered Max, holding his hands over his ears to protect them from the fiend's voice.

"Really, you expect me to believe that the great-great-great-grandson of my most hated enemy doesn't know what I'm talking about? Well, Minerva, how about you? Can you tell me where the Enotslived Diamond is? If you do, maybe I won't snap your baby brother's neck," hissed the Zarmaglorg, his forked tongue darting in and out of his monster mouth. Then he swiftly grabbed Max by the throat and squeezed. His black nails dug into Max's neck, cutting off his oxygen supply, turning his face blue.

"Stop it! Please, stop it. I'll tell you anything you want. Please!" I cried.

"I want what was inside that Bewilder Box, and I want it now! Tell me where it is or your brother dies!" The Zarmaglorg squeezed Max harder.

"I don't have what you're talking about, but I think I know where it is," I said.

"You 'think' you know where it is? Think harder. This is not a game, Minerva McFoolish!" screamed the evil king.

"Okay, okay, I'll tell you, but first let him go."

"Very well. Last chance, child," said the Zarma-glorg as he released his grip. Max gasped and gulped for as much air as he could get back into his lungs with a panicky, coughing wheeze.

"I think what you want was around the neck of our friend, Mr. Devilstone, but the Snargle ate him," I told the beast.

"You expect me to believe that? Lies, lies and more lies, child. You leave me with no choice but to kill your—"

"No!" I interrupted him before he could snap off my brother's head. "Listen to me. I swear, I'm not lying to you. Your stupid Snargle slave ate it."

"Girl sister is telling truth, master. Me filled Snargle tummy with a hurting coyote," the Snargle groaned to its master, holding its swollen, aching belly. "Snargle needs girl sister boy brother meat to cure Snargle tummyache. Master, please help me tummy hurt no more."

"Snargle, dear sweet Snargle, your tummy really is hurting you," cooed the Zarmaglorg sooth-ingly. "I've been such a bad king. Let me help you, Snargle."

"Thank you, master, thank you," said the

relieved Snargle happily, with an enormous smile upon its face. The Zarmaglorg's dark eyes crackled with evil energy, and he pointed one of his taloned fingers toward his servant, emitting a burning blast of heat. The Snargle exploded into thousands of thick, moist, meaty pieces. We were sopping wet from head to toe with Snargle gore. It was a smorgasbord for the Swoggler, who found the fresh raw bits of Snargle delicious in every way. The Zarmaglorg laughed so hard that his horns almost fell off his hideous head. I couldn't help myself; I projectile-vomited at the ungodly sight of it all, and the Swoggler swoggled that up too.

So that he didn't have to bend over, the evil king used one of his long, spiky monster toes to sort

through some of the bigger hunks of steaming Snargle mess in search of what was left of its stomach. He kicked over pieces of bone and guts, stepping into parts of brain and heart, which squished up between his toes. Finally, directly under what could have been the Snargle's liver or an undigested part of Mr. Devilstone, the Zarmaglorg discovered a faint red light shining through a thick puddle of fresh Snargle fluids. The evil king hissed with glee when he spotted what he had been missing.

"Now that I have my diabolical diamond back, I don't need to keep either of you alive." The Zarmaglorg cackled with mischief in his eyes.

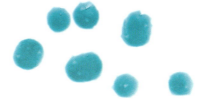

A Monstrous Miracle

*T*his was it, the end of the road for Max and me, but I didn't want to die. So I did what any smart McFearless girl from Whistlesqueak would do in a situation like this: I appealed to the Zarmaglorg's monstrous ego.

"Please, oh mighty, all-powerful king of evil, the scariest and most fearsome creature ever to walk the earth, before you eat us, I have one last question."

The Zarmaglorg stopped staring murderously upon us and twitched his head in amusement as he listened to my words of wicked praise. I hoped that I could take his mind off eating us just long enough for a miracle to happen, that somehow Max and I could think up a way to save ourselves in the short amount of time we had left.

"Yes, McWorthless, speak up. Ask what you will of me," said the Zarmaglorg with egotistically open ears.

"Thank you, oh master of my demise, the most brilliant beast of all monsterkind. I'll ask my last lowly human question," I continued. "Well, you see, I keep wondering why the most magnificent monster monarch of all time would need to blow up one of his most faithful followers for a mere diamond. What could you possibly need it for when you are already all-powerful?"

"Well, everything you say about me is true, and I'm glad that you recognize all my incredible evil attributes. Although I do need this diamond, I don't want you two thinking any less of me, because, after all, only my brilliant monster mind can conceivably understand exactly what the Enots-lived Diamond's true powers are. Now that I have it back, every last human child shall be eaten, starting with both of you. No one will be safe. Every living thing on this planet shall have to kneel before the monstrous might of me," the Zarmaglorg ranted rejoicingly.

"Yes, it is true; we don't stand a chance. No one does, your evil eminence," I said, further inflating his already huge monster head.

"It is so great to hear you say that. You know, I might actually miss you after I eat you, Minerva. I really think I will. But I can't wait to unleash the Enotslived's powers—powers that I never got to let loose fully upon this mortal world of men because of your great-great-great-grandfather Maximillius McFearless."

I might have imagined it, but I could have sworn that the moment the Zarmaglorg spoke my great-great-great-grandfather's name aloud, the red diamond in his hand reacted with a slight pulse of power, which went unnoticed by everyone except me.

"Maximillius got lucky, that's all, for no mere human truly stands a chance against my monster might. However, your ancestor managed to steal this diamond of destruction, along with that traitorous book, before I could enact my dreadful plans of domination. I have no worries anymore, though, now that it's mine once again, and very soon there won't be any more McFearlesses left to stop me. I truly do wish you could be here to see me use it to open a doorway between our two worlds, yours and the demonic dimension from which I come. You see, it was quite by accident that the diamond brought me here thousands of years ago, before I knew how to use the Enotslived's powers or even knew what they were. It teleported me here, and to my delight, I found you humans to be absolutely delicious. I grew tired of having to bring my fellow monsters here one by one and tried without any luck to create a permanent doorway between our two worlds. But after countless years of experimenting with the Enotslived's many powers, I finally discovered a way. Maximillius, unfortunately, ruined everything. Tonight, however, nothing can stop me. My nefarious plan shall finally be realized. I'm going to bring forth an army of undead demons from my dimension. I will rule your world with an evil iron-clawed fist. The entire human race will be enslaved and used as lunch meat for me and my kind. And I will force children, like you, to watch as I murder helpless puppies, for the sole purpose of collecting the traumatized tears that drip from their crying eyes in pretty goblets made from human skulls. In fact, I'll drink their salty sorrows as if they were fine wine and delight in their suffering. It's going to be great! Sadly, you'll be dead by then. It really has been fun talking to you, Minerva, but now I believe it's time that I devoured you and your brother," declared the king of evil joyously, eyes energized for death.

No more stalling. This was *really* the end for Max and me. We backed as far away as we could from the Swoggler and from the Zarmaglorg's advancing monster footsteps, until we were cornered by unclimbable cave walls that left no room for us to escape.

"Max, I want you to know that I love you and

that you're a good brother, the best brother," I said, teary-eyed, holding him tightly.

"You too, Minerva," Max said, shaking with fear. We couldn't come up with a way out of this jam, so we closed our eyes.

But then a monstrous miracle happened. Within the Zarmaglorg's hand, the Enots-lived Diamond brightened with a powerful red light. We could see its bright glow even through our closed eyelids. The Zarmaglorg screamed in pain. His wail was so horrific that we opened our eyes and had to cover our ears. The howling evil king tried to shake the damaging diamond loose from his clawed hand before it caused him any more agony, but he failed. It burnt a circular wound right through the center of his palm, cauterizing demon flesh as it passed through monster muscle and bone.

Monsters from above heard their suffering master's scream and came rushing down the stony stairs to his aid. Snarling, growling, hissing and hating creatures piled by the dozens into the room, where they too were about to bear witness to an unbelievable phenomenon.

Magically, the Enotslived Diamond floated in midair, blazing like a walnut-sized supernova. Scarlet light poured over us, with a glow that penetrated and pulled at our bodies like a weird vacuuming wind. The messy remains of the murdered Snargle that were still stuck to us and every last chunk that the Swoggler hadn't yet eaten were magically drawn into the pulsing red core of the crimson diamond and absorbed, feeding it, causing the light waves it emitted to grow even brighter and refract throughout Castle Doominstinkinfart. Its rays affected everything they illuminatingly came in contact with. Dead, burnt bats were reanimated and took flight once again with sonar-filled songs of joy. The fiery depths rumbled and rocked in anger, demanding that the light be stopped, shaking the cavern walls, causing all of us to fall to our knees.

Rats, worms and cockroaches crawled up through the foundation and circled in celebration from the happiness the red light brought to their tiny pest brains. Ms. Monstranomicon grew healthier too. Vital ink flowed back into her, and between her hardened cover brimmed freshly grown, crisp pages of parchment. Her worn, weathered, wrinkled spine smoothed over until she shone like the day she had been printed.

Max and I also had

positive reactions to the ruby rays of light. We stood brimming with life, healed of our wounds, basking in the diamond's glow. Our feelings of fear and despair had been dashed away, replaced with a McFearless desire to fight back and kick some monster butt.

The evil beings all around us, however, were suffering as if the sun had risen upon them. Clawbsterdons began boiling inside their own lobsterlike shells. Hundreds of tiny Icklickers were squealing in pain and exploding all over the place like kernels of popping corn. Unihorned Poozwampits started shaking uncontrollably and belching out gutwheezing chartreuse plumes of smoke. It was as if all of the monsters were being punished for every wicked deed they had ever done in their monstrous lives—and it was glorious.

✦ The Clawbsterdon ✦

These giant-eyed, six-armed, carnivorous crustaceans are powerfully strong creatures with bone-crushing pincers. They have nearly indestructible outer shells, which work to their advantage since they're also the most accident-prone species of the entire monster kingdom. Clawbsterdons are self-centered, opinionated, overly talkative creatures who like to remind their fellow monsters constantly just how perfect they think they are and why everyone should be in love with them. This makes them also the most unpopular breed of monster. Equally happy on land and underwater, Clawbsterdons have the amazing ability to create extraordinarily detailed mansions for themselves out of coral, sand and seashells. Preferring to build on unpopulated stretches of beach during low tide, Clawbsterdons will spend vast amounts of time working on their homes only to have them demolished by strong ocean waves at high tide, forcing them in absolute frustration to start all over. For fun, they enjoy capsizing boats full of people, destroying lighthouses and training fish to dance. Human children, preferably uncooked, highly salted and wrapped in seaweed, are a Clawbsterdon's favorite meal.

A defensive recipe:
THE MAGIC BUTTER CHARM

You will need:

- ⚓ 1 cauldron (or large mixing bowl)
- ⚓ 1 pair of human hands
- ⚓ 1 stick of butter
- ⚓ 1 lemon
- ⚓ 20 inches of red string

Place the stick of butter in your cauldron or large mixing bowl and smush it into a ball with human hands. Then squeeze the lemon over it, making sure to cover the entire ball of butter with juice. On a long, flat surface, stretch the red string into a straight line. Remove the ball of butter from your cauldron and place it in the middle of the string. Next, securely wrap the string around the butter ball three times in three different directions. Then say these magic words: *Boiling, broiling, spoiling Clawbster, magic butter destroy Clawbster.* Immediately tie the two loose ends of the red string around your neck. For one full year of Clawbsterdon protection, wear the Magic Butter Charm until it melts off. ▩

THE ICKLICKER

These incredibly small yet hugely evil creatures are the monsters that most widely populate the planet and make up the species most successful at infiltrating human domiciles undetected. These cockroach-sized creeps do so by way of their unique camouflaging capabilities. Icklickers can bend light and shadows around their miniature, hairless bodies, enabling them to create illusions powerful enough to fool the eyes of almost any human being. They have been known to cleverly disguise themselves as tiny objects commonly overlooked by humans, such as crumbs, pebbles or pieces of fuzz—or, in rare circumstances, insects, such as ants, gnats or silverfish. Since humans usually don't feel threatened by these tiny things, Icklickers have the freedom to move about in plain sight. They rove in packs and quickly infest whole houses at once, building their Icklicker hovels inside cabinetry, cracks in walls or ceilings, and any hard-to-reach places difficult for humans to clean. Once they have achieved total infestation of a house, they begin to feast upon the blood of their helpless sleeping human hosts. Icklickers work together, swarming the snoozing victims, covering them from head to toe like a blanket of death. It can take months for a swarm of Icklickers to completely drain and kill a human, leaving them free to breed and multiply before moving on to another household just down the road. Together they are a powerful force to be reckoned with, but singularly they are the easiest of monsters to defend against or kill. The lightest touch can crush their tiny frames and end their terrible, blood-sucking lives. And if humans were to take even the simplest of precautionary measures, they could be completely Icklicker-free. Humans should definitely beware of these miniature monsters.

A defensive recipe:

SOLDIER SLIMERS

You will need:

- 1 pair of human hands
- 1 bare foot for stomping and smashing
- 1 mouth for sucking up and spitting sprays
- 1 giant jar of pickles
- 1 bottle of milk

Using both human hands, open the jar of pickles. Place 1 pickle in front of every door in your home that leads to the outside of your house. (Make sure they are closed.) Using the bare foot, stomp on each pickle 13 times until properly smashed. Repeat for every door. Next, suck up a mouthful of milk from the bottle and spit it out in a nice steady spray all over every window in your home until they are completely soaked. (Make sure they are closed beforehand.) Once every entrance an Icklicker might use to gain entry into your house has been covered, say these magic words: *Icky, icky, licky, licky, curdled milk gone bad, gone sticky. Pickle power, slime and protect, transform into soldiers, yuck and condiment.* Unlike other defensive monster recipes, once performed correctly, Soldier Slimers never wear off and will keep a home Icklicker-proof for all eternity.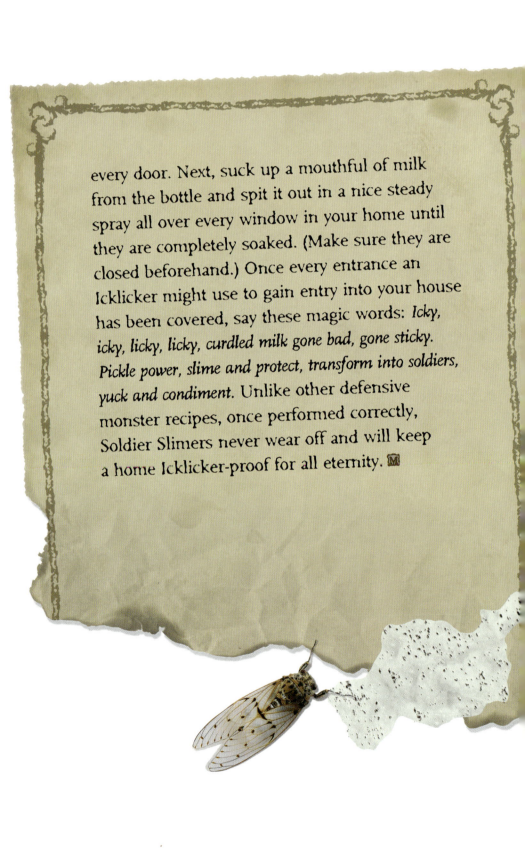

The Unihorned Poozwampit

These vicious, cloven-hoofed tricksters are a sneaky, vile breed with magical horns that protrude from the tops of their skulls. As Unihorned Poozwampits grow older, their horns get longer and their magical powers grow stronger. A Poozwampit's horn gives it the ability to move objects with its mind, turn invisible at will and grant a victim three wishes. (It is always unwise to agree to a Unihorned Poozwampit's wish-fulfilling offer, because the granted wishes always come with a heavy price.) They have a horrible desire to use their powers to torture mankind and think making mischief is hilarious. If ever a human takes a terrible tumble for no apparent reason, chances are an invisible Unihorned Poozwampit was the cause. They love to play pranks and to injure their victims before devouring them. It is incredibly difficult to outsmart a Unihorned Poozwampit, and humans should avoid this type of monster and its shenanigans at all costs. Unihorned Poozwampits' favorite foods are vanilla ice cream and penguin ravioli. They hate fruits of all kinds. They are especially terrified of spelling contests.

A defensive recipe:

PAJAMA LOAF TELESCOPE

You will need:

- 1 cauldron (or large mixing bowl)
- 1 large wooden spoon
- 1 pair of human hands
- 49 blades of grass
- 1 cup of cranberry juice
- 1 cup of cream
- 1 cup of marmalade
- 1 kiwifruit
- 1 pair of pajamas
- 1 large unsliced loaf of bread
- 3 18-inch pieces of green yarn
- 1 garden snail
- 1 timepiece for measuring time

Place the grass, cranberry juice, cream and marmalade into your cauldron or large mixing bowl. Stir it all together with the wooden spoon until the grass is thoroughly soaked and completely covered. Say these magic words as loud as possible: *Unihorn, pumpkin burn, yellow melon, mango. Red fruit, possum soup, unihorn, no fang no.* Then, using human hands, smush up the kiwifruit and drop the smushed bits into the mixture. Stir it with the wooden spoon for 1 minute. Say these magic words as quietly as possible: *Poozwampit, bamshampit, tomatoenails, pizango lama.* Now add the pair of pajamas to your cauldron and stir them all around, allowing them to absorb the contents of the cauldron. Set it aside and let it soak for 9 minutes. Next, take the large unsliced loaf of bread and, with human hands, carefully tunnel out an eyehole all the way through the center of the bread. Remove the properly soaked pajamas from the cauldron and carefully wrap them around the loaf without covering the eyehole. Fasten the pajamas securely to the bread using the pieces of green yarn. Finally, place the garden snail on top of your head and say these magic words: *Poozwampit, bamshampit, tomatoenails, pizango. Unihorn, pumpkin burn, yellow melon, no fang no no, lama.* Not only will the Pajama Loaf Telescope keep an entire family safe from Unihorned Poozwampits for a year, it will also allow its user to see a Poozwampit when it has turned itself invisible.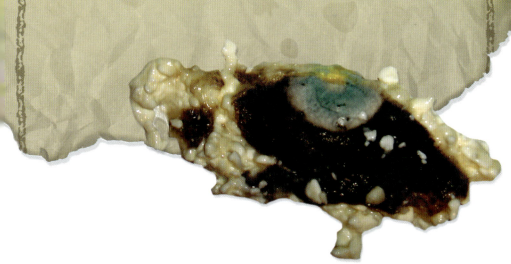

But that was not the most miraculous thing to happen by far. Something was waking up within the Enotslived—something the Zarmaglorg wasn't liking one bit. The diamond began growing, transforming, molding itself into something else, familiar yet different. A fluid form started taking shape, resembling a human baby, then reassembling itself into a coyote cub. Paws became the hands of an older boy, and hairless feet grew fur. It couldn't make up its mind, struggling with what it wanted to be. Its one-eyed animal snout contorted into the face of a one-eyed man. The glowing nebulous mass fought with itself; man or animal, it needed to decide. Finally, it must have made up its mind, because from the center of the conflicted being blasted an enormous burst of light, brighter than any we'd seen before, blinding all of us in the room, monster and human alike, with its decision. Then, all at once, everything went dark.

McFearless Once Again

"Hello, Minerva. Hello, Max. I trust that you're feeling better. Sorry it took me so long to get here," said the figure in the dark.

"Uh, who are you?" I asked.

"Minerva, don't you recognize my voice? It's me, Mr. Devilstone," replied the figure, sounding slightly annoyed.

After the blinding display of lights I had witnessed, my eyes needed time to readjust to the gloomy glow of the flames from the bottomless pit. Once they did, I recognized who was talking to me, but he wasn't who he said he was. Standing in the center of us all, surrounded by angry, injured monsters of various breeds still reeling from the burning effects of the diamond's dazzling light, was the Zarmaglorg's most hated enemy. Our great-great-great-grandfather Maximillius McFearless lived once again! He stood dignifiedly dressed, with an eye patch over his right eye, just like the

one he had in the painting above our fireplace back at home. The Enotslived Diamond rested in the center of his palm.

"I thought you said you were Mr. Devilstone," said Max, confused.

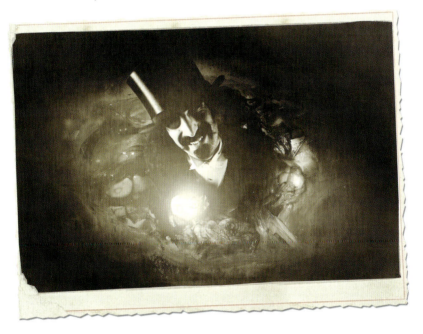

"Mr. Devilstone and I are one and the same, Max. I thought that at least one of you would have figured it out by now, that you would've put two and two together and discovered my little secret. It really wasn't that hard, considering that *Enotslived* spelled backward is *Devilstone* and that we both have only one eye."

"But how? How did you survive? How are you still alive?" I asked.

"Yes, how did you survive, McFearless?" the Zarmaglorg asked with murderous intent, staring at Maximillius through the hole in his crippled hand.

"Sorry about your hideous hand, old chum. I wish I could have taken the whole arm off, but I was a little preoccupied. Next time, I promise," answered Maximillius sarcastically.

"I can see now where Minerva got her sense of humor, and I'm not amused. Tell me how you survived all these years. Humans don't normally live that long, but then again, you're not human anymore, are you, Maximillius?" said the Zarmaglorg with a demonically smug smile upon his face. "Ah, the irony of it all. The diamond has turned you into one of us."

"No, fiend, I am nothing like you," snapped Maximillius defensively. "I may no longer be human and I may be more monster than man, but I'm no enemy to the human race. I don't cowardly devour helpless children and eat the flesh of mortals like you do, creature. I've become something worse, something that you should be very afraid of. You see, for me to survive, I must eat the flesh of monsters, and I liked what I tasted in you, Zarmy. Years ago I came here in search of knowledge, to find a way to destroy the monsters that plagued my family and so many others. I had heard legends of an ancient book, within a fortress made of tomb-stones, under the rule of an evil king. Its many pages held all of monsterkind's secrets and weaknesses, and therein lay my hopes for a safer world. Everyone told me it was suicide, sneaking into the king of evil's forbidden lair. But I had to risk it and so became the first person poisoned by the book's painful bite. As I lay here dying, I heard her voice, and she begged me to help her escape from your cruel reign. She told me all about the place from whence you came, and about how this world was in jeopardy. She said she knew things that weren't written in her pages, things that she had secreted away from you, and she offered me a choice. If I promised to take her away from this horrid place and keep her safe for all time, she would save my life, transform me. Otherwise, I would die here in this castle. So a deal was struck between us. She instructed me to pick up your precious diamond and used her knowledge of arcane incantations to fuse the diamond's hidden energies to my soul, binding us together, forever, into something unlike anything our two worlds had ever known. You discovered me lying on the floor and thought me helpless, but really I was in the beginning stages of my transformation, in a cocoonlike state, catatonically unaware of your approaching threat.

The moment you tried to finish me off, the protective powers of the diamond unleashed their full fury upon you. I'm sure you remember what happened next, beast. It must have taken you years to get out of that burning quagmire I sent you into," said Maximillius, pointing at the pit.

"Yes, as a matter of fact it did, and the pain you caused me shall never be forgotten, McFearless. I plunged horns-first into the pit's searing flames, its unholy fires licking at my monster flesh, roasting me like an evil marshmallow. I desperately swam through the pit's molten heat. It was hatred that kept me going, my hatred for you, McFearless. Eventually, I made it to the scalding rocks on the side of the pit and slowly managed to crawl, inch by agonizing inch, out of the inferno. So severe were my injuries that it took me twenty years to properly heal, with every moment of my agony a reminder of how much I hated you. The thought of exacting my revenge upon you, and upon anyone you cared for, gave me the strength to painfully carry on. I promised myself that, once fully restored, I would personally see to it that the entire McFearless family bloodline was snuffed out. I'd get my stolen diamond back and open the gateway between our worlds. I will not fail a second time, McFeeble. I will have the powers of my diamond back, and if that means having you as my slave, then so be it," the king of evil growled, signaling his minions to follow him as he charged toward Maximillius.

"Take cover, children!" commanded Maximillius over the din of vicious snarls and howls; then he quickly handed me Ms. Monstranomicon before racing straight toward the onslaught of his swarming enemies. They all collided with him at once, with the Zarmaglorg drawing first blood. The evil king pummeled our great-great-great-grandfather with a series of energized concussive blows that shook the entire castle keep. Maximillius tried to dodge other savage attacks from the ravaging creatures that surrounded him. They piled on top of him, fangs bared and razor-sharp claws slashing, smothering him under the weight of their many monster bodies. Max and I ducked behind a crop of stalagmites that protruded up near the back of the cave. It seemed impossible, from where we watched, huddled together, that Maximillius could survive something as terrible as this. It sounded like he was being torn limb from limb by the battling beasts, but against all odds, he wasn't.

With the strength of a hundred men, he emerged from the pile of the Zarmaglorg's minions, punching and kicking with fury. One by one, creatures fell as he fought them with bone-crushing force. The monsters' howls of rage and confident battle cries were rapidly replaced by wails of pain.

But that didn't stop the beasts from attacking him in droves. Maximillius shot beams of tornadoing light from his fingertips at the multiplying rush of monsters. The beams swirled around like angry wasps, instantly turning some of the creatures to ash and sending others flying about the cavern.

"You can't go on fighting like this forever, McFearless," the Zarmaglorg shrieked as he dispatched more of his evil army. "There are just too many of us. Eventually, you'll run out of power and your strength will wane, giving me the upper claw!"

"You'd like that, wouldn't you, horn head?" Maximillius answered, sending a series of red lightning bolts zapping down on the Zarmaglorg's head, frying off one of his horns with a sizzling snap that infuriated the evil king even further. However, the king was right. Because for every three creatures Maximillius monsterminated, one would land a powerful blow that left our great-great-great-grandfather visibly weaker. Still, Maximillius stood his ground and continued to fight, doling out his brand of swift justice, until all that was left of his enemies was a one-horned Zarmaglorg, surrounded by piles of the defeated.

"It's time we ended this conflict once and for all," declared an exhausted Maximillius.

"Yes, let's!" agreed the evil king

assuredly, his hate-filled eyes crackling once again with demonic power. Then the Zarmaglorg shot tendrils of chaotic magic from his hands straight up into the air and brought them arcing down upon Maximillius like a flock of carrion birds descending upon a fresh kill. Maximillius barely had time to form a protective shield of blazing light around his entire body as the dark energies coalesced upon him, battering him violently. It then became a battle of wills and ancient magic, Maximillius's crimson aura of light clashing against the Zarmaglorg's beams of crackling black. Their magics swirled and snapped at one another in the air above their heads, as if dancing to death's final lullaby. They collided like cobras, again and again, causing brilliant displays of white-hot sparks to shower down. Maximillius began buckling under the strain of the Zarmaglorg's wicked assaults. Finally, he fell to his knees.

"The world will be mine, McFearless! You've lost. Now you and the rest of your pathetic McFearless clan shall die!" proclaimed the Zarmaglorg victoriously. Maximillius was spent. He didn't breathe or even twitch. But just to make sure of his victory, the evil king sent another crippling round of magical bursts pounding down upon his hated enemy. The fight was over. All was lost, and our hearts sank. The Zarmaglorg approached the limp,

defeated body of our great-great-great-grandfather to retrieve his long-awaited prize, the Enotslived Diamond.

But the king of evil was met with a surprise.

Somehow, miraculously, Maximillius slowly and shakily rose toward his foe, veins bulging from the pressure of simply standing. "I'm not dead yet, you ugly, overgrown wart with wings—but *you* will be!" he wheezed. Then, with all the remaining strength he could muster, pulling from the very fibers of his magic-infused soul, he sent a blazing blast of unparalleled magnitude hurtling toward the cold black heart of the Zarmaglorg. This was the last thing that the evil king ever could have imagined possible. His startled scream of shock was cut short as the full force of Maximillius's attack blew a gaping hole

through his chest, tearing him in two. Both halves of the wounded Zarmaglorg's torso flopped and twitched about while he struggled without any luck to reattach them with the use of his fleeting black magic.

"This can't be happening. I'm the king of evil, and evil never dies!" the Zarmaglorg sputtered, spitting out thick gobs of rancid-smelling blood from the back of his gurgling throat. The same putrid vital fluids seeped out of his injuries, while his equally essential magical energies drained from his open wounds as well. His normally sharklike black eyes turned white as the last embers of his evil life force finally died out.

Maximillius collapsed, completely drained from the battle.

It Swoggles the Mind

*O*nly the sounds of bat squeaks filled the cave as Max, Ms. Monstranomicon and I came out of our hiding place and walked toward Maximillius. We circled him. Holding my nose with one hand and gripping my crying book friend in the other, I stood between Maximillius and the fetid remains of the Zarmaglorg. I bent down to see if the Zarma-glorg was truly dead, but before I could even touch him, Maximillius's hand reached out and grabbed my ankle, scaring all of us half to bits.

"Stay away from him. His residual energies of dark magic can still kill you. Whatever you do, don't touch his body," said Maximillius weakly.

"Yikes, okay," I replied, moving away from the dead, yet still deadly, evil king.

"I knew you weren't dead," said Max.

"Yes, but I'm barely alive. Now, listen to me, children. I must apologize for something before I pass out," said Maximillius between ragged,

wheezing breaths. "I want you to become great monster hunters, and you're both definitely well on your way. But I wasn't honest with you as to what my real intentions were from the beginning of this awful trip. I used both of you so that I could gain access to this castle unsuspected. I've been manipulating things within the shadows of the McFearless family for years. It was I who arranged for my beloved Ms. Monstranomicon to mysteriously show up on the doorstep of our family home all those years ago, establishing her safekeeping throughout the generations. When I learned that the Zarmaglorg was still alive, I realized I would need help, so I used my powers to create the illusion of a red moth and orchestrated Max's finding the secret McFearless monster study. I needed you both to meet Ms. Monstranomicon so that you could start learning early what it truly takes to be a McFearless, because I knew that your father wasn't going to teach you anytime soon. And last of all, it was I who placed myself inside the Bewilder Box and arranged for Milgrew to deliver me to your door, knowing full well that you both would find me. The Zarmaglorg's forces of evil were rising once again, and I hadn't had contact with any monster other than Ms. Monstranomicon for eons, so my powers had been severely weakened. Regrettably, I wasn't strong enough to help your father the

night the monsters surprise-attacked us. It wasn't until Max bled on me that I was able to reconstitute a body for myself. Tasting some McFearless blood fully charged what was left of my human side and enabled me to create a body with which to go forth into battle. I picked the form of a coyote, knowing full well that the Snargleflougasaurus who had attacked us wouldn't be able to resist swallowing me if it ever got the chance, and when the opportunity arrived, I let the two of you get captured. Once I was inside the Snargle's belly, I knew that I'd be able to grow even stronger. I siphoned off its monster energies while it carried me inside itself, undetected, into Castle Doominstinkinfart. I knew that as long as the Zarmaglorg believed either of you to possess the Enotslived Diamond, I would finally get my chance to destroy his evil once and for all. I never expected to grow as proud or as fond of both of you as I have. I knowingly put you directly in danger, and for that I am so sorry. I hope you can forgive me and can find your father before it's too late."

"I can't believe it. You used Max and me like puppets," I said, outraged. "You really are more of a monster than a man."

"Yes, and I understand if you hate me. But right now you must get out of here before this whole castle comes crashing down. Head for the stairs, find your father and escape this evil place. Please." It seemed there was still something left of our great-great-great-grandfather's human, compassionate side.

"Wait, we're not leaving without you. We can all go together. I'll help you," said Max.

"No. Leave me. Hurry now, go. . . ." Maximillius wheezed as he spoke his last words.

"No! Please don't die. You promised to protect me. No!" moaned Ms. Monstranomicon mournfully.

"It's okay. Max and I will protect you now," I said, trying to soothe her. But to be honest, I was a little worried about how we would escape without Mr. Devilstone's—I mean Maximillius's—help.

The three of us stared down at him for a long moment before saying our goodbyes. Ms. Monstranomicon finally stopped her sobbing in my hands as we headed toward the tiny stone steps in the distance. We had to climb over the burnt remains of many monsters to do so, but eventually we made it to the stairwell. It was impossibly dark inside, and we had nothing to light our way. We didn't know how far we would have to climb or what, if any, untold dangers lurked ahead. All we knew was that our father and our freedom lay somewhere up the steps, so we moved upward, in the dark.

Unfortunately, we didn't get very far. From the shadows leapt the cowardly Swoggler. It had been hiding all this time, afraid of Maximillius's powers,

worried that it would meet the same fate as so many of its dead master's slaves. But now it recognized an opportunity. The Swoggler smacked me hard into the side of the stairwell with a swat from four of its octopus-like sucker tentacles and snatched Ms. Monstranomicon from my grip. Then it hacked a sickeningly gluey slimeball out of its saber-toothed mouth directly into Max's face and pushed him down the stairs while it slither-ran right past him toward the pit.

"The Swoggler got Ms. Monstranomicon! What do we do now?" Max asked, rubbing Swoggler gunk from his eyes.

"Well, we're two McFearlesses against one monster, and that disgusting creature needs to be taught a lesson," I said, tired of being scared and fed up with being pushed around. "We've beaten bigger before, so I figure we can monsterminate that leeching worm once and for all. Let's go get our friend back!"

"I agree. Look for something that we can use against it," Max suggested. We scanned our surroundings, and all we could find were rocks. So we hurriedly picked up as many as we could and quickly ran after the Swoggler, in hot pursuit.

"SSssopen SSssup SSssyour SSssmind SSssto SSssme. SSssI SSsswill SSsshave SSssall SSssyour SSssecretsSS, SSsstraitor. SSssI've SSsswaited

SSsshundredsSS SSsssof SSssyearsSS SSsssfor SSssa SSsssmoment SSsslike SSsssthisss, SSsssand SSssI SSsssshall SSssfinally SSsssbecome SSssthe SSsssnew SSssking SSsssof SSssevil!" screamed  the Swoggler at Ms. Monstranomicon in frustration. It had never tried swoggling a talking book before and was having a hard time of it. The creature had her completely in its mouth and was practically sucking her cover off when the first of our rocks slammed into its head.

"Give me back my friend!" I yelled.

"SSssstay SSssback," threatened the Swoggler with its mouth full. It didn't enjoy the second or third direct hit that we fired off into its leeching wormy skull either. "SSssor SSssI'll SSssdrop SSssher SSssinto SSssthe SSsspit." Then the Swoggler took her out of its mouth and held her over the side by one of its tentacles.

"Help me, Minerva! Oh, please, Max, save me!" cried Ms. Monstranomicon, disgusted by her abductor's creepy, clammy clutches.

"Let her go, sucko!" I shouted at it even more angrily, and noticed that Max had stopped throwing rocks, which was weird because he's a much better shot. He had an odd, overly thoughtful expression on his face, and he pulled me close.

"Minerva, I have a plan. When I take my third step toward the Swoggler, drop to the ground immediately. On my third step. Remember. Okay?" Max whispered in my ear. I nodded, and then he shouted to the Swoggler, "Okay, we won't throw any more rocks at you. I want to make a trade. You give my sister back her book buddy and I'll let you taste what's in my brain."

I was shocked by what Max had said.

"SSssnever! SSsswhen SSssI'm SSssdone SSsssucking SSssevery SSssword SSssout SSssof SSssher, SSssthen SSssyou SSsscan SSsshave SSssher SSssand SSssher SSssempty SSsspagesSS SSssback SSssto SSsswrite SSsson," threatened the Swoggler, with gross sucking sounds behind every word it spoke.

"Max, what are you doing?" I shouted at him.

"Minerva, shut up," he snapped, and stared at me with a "stick to the plan; I have everything under control" look on his face. Then he turned back toward the Swoggler. "I have so many memories stuck in my head that probably taste like chocolate pudding. It would be a shame for you never to get to sample them. Have you ever even had chocolate pudding? It's my favorite. Just take Ms. Monstra-nomicon away from the pit and I'll give you a little taste," Max said, and took one obvious step closer to the Swoggler.

"SSsswell, SSssit SSssdoesss SSsssound SSsstempting," the Swoggler said, and swallowed at the idea of what my brother might taste like. Max lowered his head ever so invitingly and took one more step closer to the creature.

"Listen, it's a fair trade. Just throw Ms. Monstranomicon toward my sister and I'll personally put my head in your mouth for you to leech away upon. Think of all the yummy things I'm ashamed of or embarrassed about. My secrets alone probably taste like creamy caramels, and if you don't like caramel, think about how fantastic my fears will taste," Max continued, laying it on thick. "Look, we're just little kids. You'll probably get the book back from Minerva again anyway. You did it once before, so you can do it again. Just throw her the book and taste my brain."

That was the deal maker. Convincing the Swoggler that it could catch us again was a stroke of brilliance on Max's part. The Swoggler raised Ms. Monstranomicon from over the pit and threw her to me.

I was nervous now. What was Max going to do?

"SSssI SSssdid SSsswhat SSssyou

SSssasked SSssof SSssme, SSssMax. SSssnow SSssstep SSssforward SSssand SSssfeed SSssme," slobbered the Swoggler, salivating uncontrollably for Max's mind.

"A deal's a deal," Max said, and took his third step, which I had been waiting for. Both of us dropped to the ground at the same time. I wasn't expecting what happened next at all, but Max sure was. The moment we hit the ground, a long, moldy green wooden spear, thrown from somewhere behind us, plunged its way right into the middle of the Swoggler's chest, stopping the creature in its tracks. The beast yelled in pain and teetered on its skinny legs, shocked and outraged that it had been tricked so easily.

Seeing my brother on the ground only a few inches away from its feet gave the Swoggler an awful idea. If it was going to die, then it wouldn't be dying alone. It was going to rip my brother apart until it breathed its last breath. I had to do something. When the Swoggler bent to grab Max, I sprang to my feet with a McFearless burst of speed and jump-kicked the Swoggler, blindsiding it and sending it over the side of the bottomless pit into the scorching flames below.

"Minerva, no! Don't!" screamed Max, horrified, but it was too late. My kick had already connected. "Why did you do that?" he asked, teary-eyed.

"To save your butt," I said, not understanding the troubled look on Max's face.

What was the problem? Why wasn't he grateful? I didn't understand why Max was so upset with me. Before I could figure it out, I was picked up by two massive green hands—the same hands that had thrown the spear into the Swoggler's chest.

"Hello, Minerva. I really wish you hadn't done that," Milgrew said somberly.

"Milgrew, I thought the Snargle killed you back on the *Adelaide*!" I said, happy to see our moldy friend. Behind him stood Mushroach and Sporak, and held carefully in Sporak's arms was my father, with a huge smile on his face.

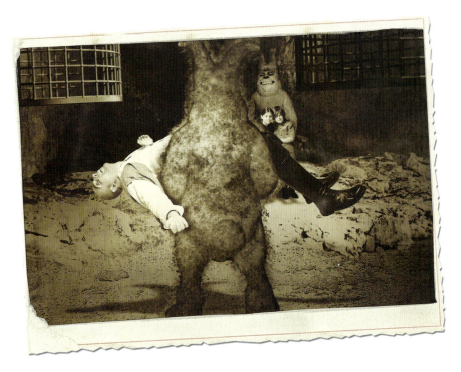

"Daddy!" I shouted with love, and ran to him immediately. I grabbed and squeezed him as hard as I could, but his stare never changed. He didn't respond to me at all. He was an empty, unfeeling shell with a cruel, contradictory smile permanently fixed on his face. It was horrible. "Why is he like this? What's going on?" I asked, scared and confused.

"When we were first fighting the Swoggler, Milgrew contacted me psychically and I told him what was happening. He said that he had our father but that Dad wasn't okay, that we needed to keep the Swoggler preoccupied until the Moldrens got here. Milgrew also explained that our father had been swoggled for too long and that we needed to be able to milk the Swoggler's monster brain to get Dad's memories back," said Max, tears rolling down his face. "We needed the Swoggler's head, Minerva, and now, since you kicked the creature over the side, Dad's going to be stuck like that forever!"

"Oh, no! I didn't know!" I cried with a dreadful sinking feeling in my gut, and sobbed into the emotionless arms of my father. "I'm so sorry, Daddy. I am so, so sorry. I just didn't know. . . ."

The Seas of Gloom

The Moldrens searched the cavern for survivors, but there weren't any. Oddly, there was also no sign of Maximillius or of the Zarmaglorg's body. In fact, lots of the monster bodies had disappeared inexplicably. Not a single live monster was left inside to bar our way, so it was easy for us to take our leave of Castle Doominstinkinfart.

For the grueling day and a half that it took for us to cross the sands of Skullbury Desert, Max wouldn't speak to me. He'd only communicate mentally with Milgrew, and he would turn his head every time our eyes met. My guilt over my father's state of mind was eating away at me. I wished that this was all just a bad dream, but I knew it wasn't.

The Moldrens cared for my father through the night, and I stayed by his side every second of the daylight hours, hoping that he'd snap out of his catatonic state. But he never did anything other

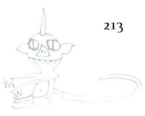

than smile that false smile of his.

When we made it to the *Adelaide,* Max didn't even get excited about seeing his own living ship or want to sail with her topside. Instead, he opted to sulk silently inside the captain's quarters, behind locked doors, and tried to keep himself from getting seasick. Mushroach and Sporak placed my father in the ship's fore cabin for his own safety, then jumped off the deck to swim ahead, preferring the anti-social calm of the waters they knew and loved. Milgrew took command of the *Adelaide* and set course for Whistlesqueak. I occasionally made idle conversation with him, but it felt kind of forced. Maybe I was paranoid, but I kept thinking that Max was saying bad things about me in Milgrew's mind while we had our chats. So it was hard for me to enjoy his company. Ms. Monstranomicon kept trying to make me feel better by telling me over and over that my father's state of mind wasn't my fault, but that only made me feel worse.

All in all, the mood that surrounded everyone aboard the ship was one of pure gloom.

That night, after I had cried for about an hour and just before the gentle rocking of the waves sent me to sleep, a feeling that I'll never get used to happened to me for the second time. The world around me ceased to exist, and once again I was moving incredibly fast without actually moving at all, hurtling through time and space into a void of pitch-black darkness. I emerged in a small candle-lit room aboard the *Adelaide.* In front of me, sitting at a small table grown directly from the floorboards of the ship itself, were Max and Milgrew. Ms. Monstranomicon was there too, happily resting in the hands of the being who had teleported me.

"Now that you are all here, let's get down to business."

It was Maximillius—in the form of Mr. Devilstone once again.

"I know a way to get your father's memories back. Max, you're going to have to stop being such a jerk to your sister, and, Minerva, stop being such a dramatic fool, or I won't help either of you," he said, and unceremoniously swatted both of us in the face with his tail.

I was so happy to see the cantankerous coyote that the shock of his tail swat and the dirty, gross-tasting mouthful of fur deposited on my tongue didn't even bother me.

"Okay, now that that's settled, can I count on

you all to help me retrieve Manfred's memories?" Mr. Devilstone asked.

"I will help," said Milgrew.

"Anything for you, sweetie," said Ms. Monstra-nomicon lovingly.

"You can count on me for sure," said Max, a smile finally returning to his face.

"Now, what about you, Minerva?" asked Mr. Devilstone, smirking, with his tail wagging back and forth impatiently.

"Of course!" I shouted, with hope restored.

Mr. Devilstone nodded. "Good. Now let's go wake your mother up."

THE END

**These are the people, places and things that, for various reasons,
I feel must be thanked from the bottom of my heart:**

My fourth-grade teacher, Tracy McDonald. Helen Breitwieser, for believing I could do it. Clay, my vegan, weirdo, genius sculptor and incredible artist of a friend, for going above and beyond. Chris Angelilli, for giving me this opportunity and for making this a much better book. Tanya Mauler and all of the other fine people at Random House, whose exceptional hard work turned my dream into a reality. You have my deepest gratitude. The Incomparable Brendan Smith. Mr. Snoobles. Keith Lawler. Shea, Jona, and Brian Bowen-Smith, for capturing the magic. Du-par's in Studio City. Paris, for your help with costumes and our late-night pancake consumptions. Anna, my Minerva McFearless. I couldn't have done this book without you. Julie, Elio, Luca, Daniel, Scruffy and a big round of applause for Elena; your love and support mean so much. Shon at Valentino's. Carolin at Nardulli. The Katlemans—Steve, Janet, Nick and Sara. My consigliere, Harris. My father, Frank, for sharing your love of monsters with me; I miss you. My mother, Gail, for calling me her favorite poet. And to the rest of my ever-growing family, Moon, Paul, little Mathilda, Dweezil, Lauren, Diva, Molly, Lizzie, Michael, Mimi, Jim and Katie. The number 8. Maurice Sendak. Apple computers. Sweet Rosa Valladares, for taking such good care of me. The Aroma Café. Tory, the funniest person on the planet, and the lovely Rose. Isky, the mysterious robot. Jules, my reptilian, worrying friend. Chuck at Rock Central. Niall, my sword-fighting, laser-shooting backyard buddy; thanks for being a part of my book. Allison, Harris, Phinneas, Bacon and Bobby. Jan, Brenna, Jack, Ana Lovelis, Kenny, Szatania, Pyrena, Mac Kinley and Draykus Enea. Both Godzillas: the giant rubber monster and my dearly departed dog. Alice Warshaw, I still owe you some monster sculptures; I hope this book makes up for it. TuTu, for her legendary grapefruit cake. Sean Larkin and Candace. David Brady, you're always there for me. Kristen, Devon and Savanna. Paul and Jerry. Tom, "The Electrician." Urth coffee, Carmel by the Sea. My fur goblin, Wink.

Last but nowhere near and definitely not the least, the biggest thanks of them all must go to my amazing wife. I never could have written this book without your support and understanding. You are my best friend, Selma, and I love you forever and ever.